WILL CANDURI

TRANSLATED BY ANDREA LABINGER

ILLUSTRATED BY MEGAN HERZART

TWISTED
CROWS

SPANISH-INFUSED SHORT STORIES

for Phillip
Enjoy The Journey!

Will
2023

Twisted Crows. First Edition: May 2023.

BPRO Editorial. Detroit, Michigan, USA.

Bproconsulting.com.

This is a work of fiction. Names, characters, places, and incidents either are the product of the author's imagination or are used fictitiously. Any resemblance to actual persons, living or dead, events, or locales is entirely coincidental.

Instagram: @willcanduri

Translated from Spanish by Andrea Labinger

translatino-translation.com

Illustrations and book cover by Megan Herzart 2023.

Instagram: @meganherzart

This book is not suitable for minors.

Translator's Note

By Andrea G. Labinger

Will Canduri's work defies categorization. To describe *Twisted Crows*, his fifth published work of fiction, as "a collection of short stories"[1] is to fall short of the mark, as the description fails to capture the enormous diversity of tone, style, setting and narrative voice represented in its pages. Twisted Crows picks up where Ensalada de Cuervos (Crow Salad) leaves off, with one story in the second volume bearing the same title as the first book: "Crow Salad." However, the complete absence of crows in the second volume is more than a little puzzling. When asked about the paucity of those birds – who are literarily linked not only to Poe's "Raven,"[2] but also to many references from Antiquity (the Biblical flood; figures from Ancient Greece and Rome; etc.), Canduri replied:

"The reason for this title is that the crow is an opportunistic animal, competitive, very intelligent, and extremely adaptable. When I wrote the eighteen tales for [my first book], many of the comments I received focused on the variety of genres included, so that [my] concept behind this anthology was to visualize each tale as a crow that tried to outdo or surpass the others [in its audacity, creativity, *et cetera*]…" Canduri also explained the meaning behind the adjective "twisted" in his fifth title: "As a writer, I enjoy using plot twists in my tales, and although it's not a device I borrow blindly, many of the short stories contain these unexpected twists and turns, for example: 'Rot in Hell, Ramón,' 'Ludovico,' 'Lanky's Helmet,' and others."

---

[1] His first book, *Ensalada de cuervos* (2021), is, similarly, a compendium of short pieces encompassing various genres and narrative styles.

[2] It is interesting to note that, although crows and ravens are *not* identical, the Spanish word for both birds is the same: *cuervo.*

Indeed, the notion of "meandering" through a lush variety of locales, eras, and genres serves to reinforce the vertiginous twisting and turning demanded of the reader of this book. From a ship on the open seas in 486 A.D. ("The Legend of the *Astronarda*") to the home of a dysfunctional family on a megaplatform in the year 2139 ("Crow Salad") to the timelessness of myth ("On the Shores of the Guatavita") to contemporary, recognizable scenarios, such as those depicted in the story "The Water I Spilled Yesterday" and the murder mystery "Where is Jack Rickshaw?", Canduri's imagination transports us – in the etymological sense of the word. His deft hand with dialogue and genre is equally remarkable. I have a special fondness for those pieces that capture the vicissitudes of the human condition under the most rigorous of circumstances: the impoverished vagrants in "Olivia and Me" (spoiler alert: Olivia is a supermarket pushcart), or the headstrong curmudgeon in "Two Rocking Chairs," who is miraculously persuaded by his grandson to make peace with his nemesis after years of a bitter standoff). Even those characters whose lives seem completely alien to our own are infused with humanity; they are always multi-dimensional, never caricatures.

As a translator, I was especially delighted to become acquainted with Will Canduri's work for the authenticity and variety of its language. He captures Cuban and Dominican street argot as effortlessly as the formality of the Gothic novel or the crispness of the traditional whodunit. It has been a pleasure to explore this "crow's-eye view" of the many worlds of Canduri's prose.

I wish you a happy journey!

"Imagination is the beginning of creation. You imagine what you desire, you will what you imagine, and at last, you create what you will."

GEORGE BERNARD SHAW

Table of Contents

Crow 1

The Water I Spilled Yesterday

By the time the image on the canvas came alive, and just before the terror was set in motion, the water had spilled, and with it, any possibility of revealing the truth of what had happened on that rainy May afternoon in 2009 in Detroit had vanished. My name is Laura; I don't use my married name. I have no idea what's going on, but I don't want to spend even one more second here.

I hear the front door close. Immediately, I climb upstairs from the basement, which is nothing but a pile of rubble, old shoes, useless clothing, and a battered wooden table, on which something resembling a carefully framed painting lies, face down. I don't want to turn it over and risk damaging it. I'd need someone else to help me, and Jason and I agreed to meet here at five, after he takes our son to an emergency specialist who's available today. No doubt they left this painting here, and there was some mishap that made them forget about me, too.

When I get to the upper floor, avoiding boards, rocks, and other left-behind objects, I grab the old doorknob with both hands. It's still stuck. I've been locked in here since four, when I showed up to do the first inspection of the house I was given as partial payment. I haven't been able to open the door since. I've banged on it with some debris I found, but it's all been useless. I hear steps outside, but at night, the downpour finds a way to keep me from identifying anything in particular. It could be just a vagrant, but I don't think so. Maybe a deer or some other animal trying to get in; it doesn't sound like a person. There are some leaks in the ceiling, allowing the water to drip down in several areas of the living room.

"Anyone out there? Could you call 911? I'm locked in here!"

No answer. I check my cell phone again, but there's still no signal.

Damn it, how will I ever get out of here? I imagine Jason must have had some sort of car problem.

I walk around randomly, stepping on the rubble with my phone in my hand. I'm trying to get some kind of signal. Using the phone, I try to light my way to the kitchen. I get a signal and quickly punch in 911.

The call can't be completed. My phone has lost its charge. Now, the real tragedy begins.

CHILD'S PLAY

It was yesterday morning at 7:45 when the alarm went off for all of us in the house. Who are all of us, you ask? Just my husband, Jason, and our eight-year-old son, Richard, were there. That time of day has remained a constant in our routine, even before Richard was born.

By the time the alarm clock goes off, I'm already awake. I've never gotten over that strange habit of waking up ahead of the clock. Ever since I was a little girl, I've been panicky about being late for anything, and in my deepest dreams, it's common for me to feel that no matter how hard I try, punctuality eludes me. It's not for nothing that I go to bed with a long, vague list of chores in mind, only to try to get up early to make sure there are no more tasks pending. Call Dilan, meet with Mrs. Barnes, buy materials for work, go to Richard's presentation, stop by the post office, the dry cleaner... Oh, well.

I use the brushes for painting. I'm not very good at that business of jotting down pending chores, like an act of faith between the paper and my worries, like my therapist, Dr. Gladstone, recommended. I've told him thousands of times: I lose Post-It notes, timetables annoy me, and calendars exhaust me. But he doesn't see it that way.

"Laura, writing down your concerns will make you feel more at ease with yourself. You should try to relax and prepare your body for some much-needed sleep."

"Doctor, if I write it down, then I'll be worrying about the Post-It note."

I've never believed in therapists. They generally turn out to be even crazier than their clients. But Jason insists on getting help ever since that episode with Richard, and to tell the truth, Dr. Gladstone seems like a good guy. Besides, stopping by his office is an excellent excuse to grab a coffee and a pineapple donut at Café Livernois. They're in the same square. Somehow, I escape into my own world and take advantage of summer to observe details that inspire me to paint. It's what I do. It's what I do best.

Of course, it's not such a problem for Jason. He sleeps with his mouth open, as though the world isn't waiting for him, or as if Richard's breakfast could make itself. I admit I'm jealous of his casualness. That's why I sleep with my back to him, since it annoys me to see how his expression of pleasure and the pillow work together in such harmony. They seem to understand one another perfectly. Maybe Jason's right, and that's why I never learned to dance. I couldn't get used to following someone else's steps. I mean, I'm not talking about rebellion in and of itself, but rather about what happens with my pillow, which sometimes behaves like a hot cement block that settles on my neck and tortures my cervical spine. Other times, when I'm trying to turn it over to enjoy its cooler side, it leaves me at the mercy of a long night of insomnia. I sleep on the right side of the bed and could move in any direction to find a comfortable corner for my body. Changing the bedspread or facing the fanciful triangular designs that the bricklayer gave the ceiling form part of that ritual of constant adjustments my body makes in protest against the mattress. Then, I turn toward Jason's satisfied expression, and it starts all over again.

Before, at least, I had the excuse of taking care of Richard. I'd get up and walk around his room to verify that he was sleeping better than either of his parents. He hardly ever woke up early in the morning complaining about anything, and when he did, he simply kicked his cradle a couple of times. I would leave our bedroom enveloped by darkness and accompanied by an assortment of gestures, yawns, and a variety of sounds designed to wake Jason. And yet, following the typical frustration his unflappable attitude caused me, I chose to turn right, leaving my slippers in the hallway so that after passing the guest bathroom, I stumbled my way into Richard's room. The baby had his eyes open, and his arms extended for me to pick him up, without any trace of anxiety or tears. Jason didn't notice a thing. They are father and son, after all.

"Okay, Mr. Lazybones, time to get up."

"Five more minutes, Mom."

"You'll be late for school. I don't want Ms. Norman to scold you again. So, let's get going to the bathroom!"

"Will you let me paint in your studio after school?"

"We'll see, we'll see. Mr. Lazybones wants to negotiate…What do you say we stop for some bubble gum ice cream first?"

"With colored sprinkles?"

"It's a deal!"

"Will you buy one for Lucas?"

"Honey, we've talked about this before…It's okay for you to have an imaginary friend, but you've got to be connected to reality."

"But Mom! Lucas will be mad if we don't get him ice cream…"

"All right, one for you and one for Lucas…"

Detroit is a great city. Or at least it will be again in the not-so-distant future. After getting into the banking business, Jason was a real estate agent for more than ten years, and to be honest, we still haven't gotten over the fact that we landed this house as partial payment for an oil painting commissioned by a very exclusive client. The house needs a lot of work, that's for sure. Besides, the area isn't habitable yet. Lots of empty houses within a five-block perimeter, most of them burned down by their owners due to the financial and real estate disaster of 2008. Facing the impossibility of paying off their mortgages, the most financially vulnerable people found it necessary to seek reparations from the insurance companies. A real mess. But Jason did a little research with some old office mates, and we now know that an important construction company has started a project to regain that sector with the help of the Michigan government.

We have just one car, which I use most of the day. I walk to school and then to Jason's work. We both agree that this is the right way to make our family wealth grow: a chance to raise awareness of my work and a secure future for Richard.

"Richard, did you pack your breakfast?"

"Peanut butter sandwiches?"

"And an apple…"

"Mom, can I take Mister Potato Head to school?"

"Promise me you'll take care of him? Jason! It's getting late!"

"I'm coming right now!" Jason replies, hurrying downstairs and fiddling with the knot of his tie.

"Dad! Mom's letting me take Mister Potato Head to school…"

"That's great, Richard! That way, you can show Super Potato's superpowers to your friends."

"Can we buy Lucas a Mister Potato Head? He's always trying to take mine away from me…"

"Sweetie," I try to reply, bending over the dishwasher.

"Your mom and I will discuss it, all right?" Jason says, interrupting me.

"Yeah!" Richard shouts, excited.

"Jason!"

"We haven't said yes…Just that we would discuss it. Now, promise me one thing, little guy: You need to tell Lucas that you're a big boy now and you can't see him all the time. Big boys have to do things that only big boys can do."

"Like taking Mister Potato Head to school?" Richard replies.

"You have to take care of Mister Potato Head. That's something only big boys do. Would you like a puppy?"

"Yes! But Lucas…Yes!"

"Great. Show us that you're a big enough boy to take care of a puppy. Now, grab your backpack and wait for us in the car."

Jumping for joy, Richard heads for the garage.

"What the hell was that all about, Jason? We've never talked about an animal in the house."

"Do you want to struggle with an invisible friend your whole life, or would you rather clean dog poop? We've got to try to get the kid to focus his attention on something else, to take on responsibilities. You have a brilliant husband, right?"

"I'm just saying we should have talked it over first. But let's go – we'll be late for school. Besides, I want you to know that he's asked to come to my studio to paint."

"What did Dr. Gladstone have to say about that?"

"He told me to let him express himself, but that I should try to give him topics to draw about. That I should communicate with him through painting and channel his fantasies that way."

"I hope the doc knows what he's doing."

"He's a psychiatrist, Jason. But I confess that it terrifies me to think it could happen again. Did you talk to Ms. Norman?"

"Yes, she's aware of the situation."

MRS. BARNES

"I've heard a lot at the golf club about your talent."

"Thanks, you're very kind."

"And that painting at Dr. Gladstone's house. It's a real inspiration for me. I admit I've visited him many times just so I could look at it. I understand from the doctor that you're a graduate of the New York School of the Arts…"

"That's right. Do you like art, Mrs. Barnes?"

"Let's say I'm a person with a great weakness for elegant décor. At my age, I'm content to have a lovely living room with a style that revolves around a focal point. The key to life is a magical point that concentrates all our desires and the experiences we've lived. A visual moment can make all the difference for a good host."

"Oh, yes…In fact, I love to portray meanings."

"Would you like something to drink? How thoughtless of me! Here we are, standing right in front of the drawing room, and I haven't ever invited you in."

"Don't worry. I'm fine."

"Come in, at least, and have a seat, dear. The fragrance will invite you to try Grandma Barnes' fabulous apple juice. Everyone comes here to have a little."

"Apples give me heartburn. A glass of water would be great, though."

Hesitantly, Laura enters a small drawing room with two antique, but very well-preserved, sofas, facing one another. In between, a coral sculpture of peonies illustrates Mrs. Barnes' intention of creating a very comfortable space for talking, having tea or the apple juice, whose properties she just praised. Placed diagonally across the corner of the room is a white bureau in an unexpected Greek style serving as the base for some decorative artifacts, including some black-and-white photos, presumably of family members, in which her absence is notable.

"Is this your family?" Laura asks Mrs. Barnes, who is now returning from the kitchen with a glass in her left hand and a glass pitcher in the other.

"The photos? Oh, yes…They're my grandchildren. Pianists, all of them. I have no idea where they inherited that artistic streak."

"I see…That explains the beautiful Steinway grand in the living room. I really identify with the fusion of minimalism and classical art…You also seem to be a virtuoso of good musical taste."

"I used to be, my dear. I played just a little. Over time, encroaching arthritis forced me to live on memories and apple juice, which you, incidentally, refuse to try."

"Those photos of your grandchildren look old, possibly from the last century. And that flame effect around the edges…Did some artist retouch them?"

"My former husband did it, but if you don't mind, I'd rather not discuss that topic."

"Oh, I'm sorry, Mrs. Barnes. I didn't know it was a sensitive topic."

"It definitely is. As I told you before, I'd like you to create an oil painting based on this photograph of my oldest grandchild, without further information."

"I'd really like to ask you to tell me a little about his life, so I can try to reflect a story behind the work, but don't worry about it. Virtuosos don't need much more to tell a story than their own music."

"Thank you for understanding. On this tape, you can hear his brilliance in interpreting Schuster."

"Oh! An audio tape! I haven't seen one of these in a long time. Don't you have a digitized file? I mean, it would make things a little easier for me."

"I'm sorry, dear. As you can imagine, we older folks don't go in for technology. But don't worry, any additional expenses you incur can be added to our final agreement of eight thousand dollars and the house on Robson Street."

"Excellent," Laura says. At the same time, she picks up the glass of water that the sweet lady had brought her a few moments earlier. "It's beautiful. The glass, I mean. Is it from the forties, or maybe the fifties? I imagine this band around the edge of the glass is gold…"

"I tend to collect this type of thing. For me, these objects live on through their beauty, but also in the stories they have to tell."

"Any story in particular?"

"What's new with Dr. Gladstone?" asks Mrs. Barnes in an attempt to change the subject.

"Excuse me for interrupting, but I think it's time for me to go. I must take care of some errands…" But as she arises from the sofa, Laura accidentally drops the glass of water, which shatters into pieces against the wooden floor. "Oh, Mrs. Barnes! How clumsy I am! But don't worry, I'll clean up this mess and pay for the glass."

"Don't you worry, Laura! These things happen. I hope I haven't overwhelmed you with my proposal."

"Not at all, Mrs. Barnes," says Laura, very nervously. "I insist you let me help you clean it up."

"No!" Mrs. Barnes categorically replies. The expression in her eyes has changed, like two flames capable of burning everything around them. "It would be best for you to go and take care of your errands."

"You have no idea how embarrassed I am. You have a very lovely home," Laura says, as Mrs. Barnes walks her to the door.

"Goodbye, Laura. It's been a great pleasure to learn more about your work. And forgive me if I overreacted about the glass."

"So long, Mrs. Barnes. I'll start working on the painting immediately and will keep you up to date on my progress."

GENIUS

After spending the entire trip talking about the refurbishing of the new house, we're greeted by an unwanted row of cars at Richard's school: our welcoming committee. I haven't had a chance to see the inside of the house yet, just some photos that Mrs. Barnes showed us. We know that, even in the worst-case scenario, the parcel of land would be an excellent acquisition.

"Jason, I think it's better if you and Richard get out and walk to the entrance. The line is very long."

"Mom, are you gonna pick me up today and get me bubble gum ice cream?"

"Yes, sweetheart. Behave today and take good care of Mr. Potato Head. Listen to everything Ms. Norman says."

"Okay, Mom!"

"How about a kiss for Mom, who's gonna buy the ice cream? I love you."

Jason climbs out of the car with Richard, as both of them walk toward the entrance of the school. Ms. Norman comes out to greet the boy. The line advances very slowly. Jason stops to chat with the teacher, while I lower the sun visor to check my makeup. I only got it halfway done before leaving home. As I look in the vanity mirror, a horrible face, disfigured by impressive burns, appears to be sitting in the back seat. I scream.

I scream very loudly and get out of the car. Jason and Ms. Norman run toward me. The drivers in front and behind my car reveal expressions of shock from their seats. I peek in the window to make sure there's no one in the back seat.

"What's wrong, Laura?" asks Jason, agitated. He takes me by the arm and peers into the vehicle.

I have nothing to say. I just cover my face and weep in despair. Terrified. Suddenly, I improvise a reply so as not to arouse Ms. Norman's suspicions.

"It's my friend, Sofía. She's died in an accident."

Jason stares at me. He understands what's happening and decides to go along with my story.

"Oh, honey, I'm so sorry. What awful news!" he says loudly, in an artificial tone directed toward everyone in line, including the imperturbable teacher.

"It's a shame. I'm so sorry for your loss," the teacher says with a certain suspicious air. "Mr. Cooper, I hope we'll be able to continue our conversation another time."

"Yes, Ms. Norman. We'll come by tomorrow to talk about what's happened," Jason replies.

I immediately wave to the teacher and get back into the car. Jason shuts my door and apologizes to the driver behind us. He straightens his tie and walks around the front of the car to get in on the passenger's side.

"Let's go," he mutters between clenched teeth, smiling at a woman who's walking along the sidewalk with her daughter, never taking her eyes off us.

Once we're outside the school grounds, I turn off the motor. I can't stop crying. I tell Jason what happened. He seems understanding, but also helpless.

"What happened with Richard? What did Ms. Norman say?"

"We'll talk about that later. Now, just calm down. If you'd like, I'll drop you off at home and take the car."

"I can't. I have to stop by Mrs. Barnes' house to close the deal on that painting."

"Hello? Mike?" says Jason after punching a number into his phone. "Listen, man…Any chance you could cover for me today on the J.P. Kingston file?"

"What are you doing, Jason?" I ask. "That's not necessary."

Looking into my eyes but otherwise not responding, he takes my arm with his left hand and replies to the person on the other end of the phone. "Yes, perfect. Just a family issue. But everything's all right. I'll be at work on Saturday. Sound good? All right…Thanks, buddy."

I sigh deeply, with a displeased expression. "Jason, why are you doing this? I don't need a babysitter…"

"It's just for today, babe. It'll help us spend a little time together."

"Jason…"

"It's Richard…Ms. Norman wants him to be evaluated more extensively. He drew some disturbing things yesterday in art class. They think he has unusual talent."

"What do you mean, *unusual talent*?" I reply, intrigued.

"He plays piano with a virtuosity that no one can explain. The teacher asked me if he's been taking music lessons at home. I told her we don't even have a piano. She said the school wants to lend him a keyboard to practice on. We need to pick it up today."

"What the hell's going on, Jason?" I stop the car again and rest my head gently on the steering wheel. "I don't know if what you're saying should make me feel happy or worried."

"Let's just follow the road and see where it leads us."

"Let's call Dr. Gladstone."

"Yes. Sounds like a good idea to me."

A LONG NIGHT

When I left Mrs. Barnes' house, I felt a little confused. I can't deny it. That elderly woman had a strange air about her. Let's say she's somewhat eclectic, which is perfectly reflected in her desires and even her decorating style.

Jason was waiting for me in the car. After running a few errands, changing drivers, and having lunch together—something we didn't do very often—he drove me to Jefferson Avenue to close the oil painting deal that the lady wanted to finalize.

"Listen, you're not gonna believe what I've got here," I said to Jason as he hopped into the car.

"Don't tell me she paid you in advance."

"No. Mrs. Barnes wants me to listen to this tape to understand a little more about the subject of the portrait."

"An audio tape? A sixty-minute TDK…It's a relic! Where will we find an audio cassette player for this thing?"

"No idea. Let me look on the internet for someplace where they can digitize the audio."

"Wait! Remember the Walkman copier you used for exercising when we were dating?"

We laughed.

"What are you talking about? Does that thing still exist?"

"In those boxes in the basement. The ones we haven't opened since our last move. I can try it to see if it still works."

"First, you've got to find it, Mr. Melrose Place."

"Don't make fun of me. You used to like to listen to music at my place with that monstrosity."

"I'd never take it outside…"

"It's just a matter of taste."

I have to admit that the idea of spending the day together was very romantic, though we still needed to return to the school to pick up Richard, with every possibility of running into Ms. Norman again.

"Did you call Dr. Gladstone?" I asked Jason.

"Yes, but I only spoke to the secretary. The soonest appointment is next week."

"God, it's so hard to get a medical appointment in this city…"

When we reached the school, as we might have expected, Ms. Norman was waiting outside with Richard.

"Hi, Ms. Norman. Hi, Sweetheart."

"I hope you're feeling better, Mrs. Cooper."

"Yes. It was just some bad news. Please, call me Laura. I don't use my married name."

"Oh, excuse me! I imagine your husband has mentioned that…"

"Yes, he did. Sweetheart, can you wait for me in the car with Dad?"

"I've got the keyboard and Mr. Potato Head!" Jason remarked.

Once they had both gotten far enough away, Ms. Norman said, "Ms. Laura, I understand that this is a complicated family situation. But Richard needs special attention."

"Ms. Norman, with all due respect, my son isn't some strange object…"

"Not at all; that's not what I mean. But we believe the boy is expressing, through his drawings, some problems that you and your husband might be having at home."

"I'm sorry, but Jason and I have a normal relationship."

"I understand your point of view, Ms. Laura. But remember, certain things that might be normal for you can be much more violent for the child."

"Ms. Norman, I won't let you suggest there's domestic violence in my family. We're very close, and we've never been aggressive toward one another."

"Don't get me wrong…But it's our duty to ask…"

"Thank you for your interest and the efforts you make with Richard. But he's being seen by the best therapist in Detroit."

"Dr. Gladstone. Yes, I know. And what about you folks?"

"What do you mean by that?"

"In cases like this, the family needs as much support as the child."

"Ms. Norman, I think that'll be all for today. Thank you."

"This is one of the drawings Richard made in art class," Ms. Norman said, showing us a sheet of paper with random streaks of watercolor paint. "In this drawing, you can see a middle-aged woman trying to set a house on fire with a man and a boy inside. And we have seven of these.

All different scenes of violence. I don't want to assume anything—that's not my job here. But in all of them, the aggressor is a woman."

"Ma'am, please avoid these insinuations. We'll deal with it," I said, taking the drawing and placing it in my purse.

That afternoon, after eating ice cream and buying another Mr. Potato Head, we arrived home around six. Jason could see the tension in my face during that time, when we couldn't talk about what was happening between the teacher and me. Just as I had promised Richard, we had a delivery pizza for dinner, and then I went downstairs to my study to begin working on some sketches, while Richard sat beside me, drawing on a little scrap of canvas that I had laid on the floor for him. Jason remained in the living room, connecting the keyboard for the child's piano practice.

"Today, we're going to have a contest. I'll start drawing this photo and you'll draw Mr. Potato Head. What do you think of that?" I said to Richard, rolling the photograph open on top of a pedestal at the boy's eye level.

Richard shook his head no.

"Okay, Son, would you like to draw me using this Walkman of Dad's while I paint?"

Richard shook his head again.

"Well, I see that our invited artist is being difficult today. What do you want to draw?"

"I want to draw the same thing as you."

"What a surprise! Richard wants to compete with his mother—a contest of equals. All right, Mr. Painter, but let's make some fair rules. We're going to give our work a name before we get started."

"Mom, why do we need to give it a name if it already has one?" the boy asked, pointing to the photo.

"What do you mean, it already has one?"

"Yeah. We're gonna draw Lucas. That's Lucas."

"Okay, enough! It's bedtime. No more contest."

"But Mom!"

"I said no!" I shouted as loud as I could.

"What's going on?" asked Jason, startled. He had gone down to the basement after the boy went upstairs in tears.

I couldn't say anything more. I just threw myself on his shoulder, crying. I couldn't paint anything that night, either. After a long conversation, Jason and I decided to go to bed. We peeked into Richard's room and saw that he had already fallen asleep.

It soon became clear that it was going to be a long night for me. I took the pills that Dr. Gladstone had prescribed and went to bed with Jason's Walkman, which we had determined to be functional. Well, halfway functional. It was important not to let the tape get tangled up. After all, it was Mrs. Barnes' tape, and in addition to the broken glass, I didn't want to damage this relic, too.

After turning off the lights and crying silently for a couple of hours, I checked to see if Jason had fallen asleep. I took the Walkman and pushed the ON button carefully to listen to the recording. Immediately, a beautiful piano interpretation began to play. I recognized it right away as the magnificent piece, *The Water I Spilled Yesterday*, by Austrian composer Leopold Schuster. It was a piece we studied in a class at art school when I was completing my studies. I enjoyed it as never before. That child was a piano virtuoso. Listening to his interpretation, I could visualize a sensitive man, very formal, and with perfect manners.

However, and as one might have expected, after a few minutes, the tape became tangled in Jason's old Walkman. Nonetheless, the music kept on playing, this time sounding closer. A chill ran down my body from head to toe. I pressed the button a few times to stop the recording, but even so, the performance continued at the same point where I had left it. Horrified, I took off my earphones and realized that the piano performance was coming from our house.

I left the room, but not without first falling and banging my head against the door. I stood up and hurriedly went downstairs. This time, Jason was awake. He ran after me.

Richard was playing the keyboard.

THE HOUSE

I walked around randomly, stepping over the rubble with my phone in my hand. I was trying to get some kind of signal. I used the phone to help light my way to the kitchen. I got a signal and quickly punched in 911.

The call couldn't be completed. My phone was out of charge. This is where the real tragedy begins.

I took the bottle of water from my purse and tried to take little sips to calm my nerves. From the kitchen, the knob on the front door began to look like it was being forced with very violent movements.

"Who's there? This isn't funny!"

No one replied. The banging grew louder. They were going to knock down the door.

In desperation, I ran downstairs, tripping over everything I encountered. I couldn't see well in the darkness. I would need to hide in the basement and find something to defend myself with.

When I reached the table where the painting lay, I had no choice but to remove the steel bar that was pressing on the work. The water bottle that had been placed on the table spilled over the dusty canvas. A white, very bright light, radiated from the canvas. Trapped by my panic, I fell on top of some old dishes in front of the table. The painting was a portrait, just like the one Mrs. Barnes had. The inscription below the portrait said, "Lucas Barnes, 1853." It all ended there.

The next day, the press and other communications media in Detroit were quite shocked. The charred corpses of Jason and Richard Barnes, ages forty-one and eight, respectively, were discovered inside their home, which had been completely destroyed by the flames. It is assumed that the author of the double homicide was visual artist Laura Barnes, who was also discovered by police hanged in the basement of an abandoned residence on Robson Avenue.

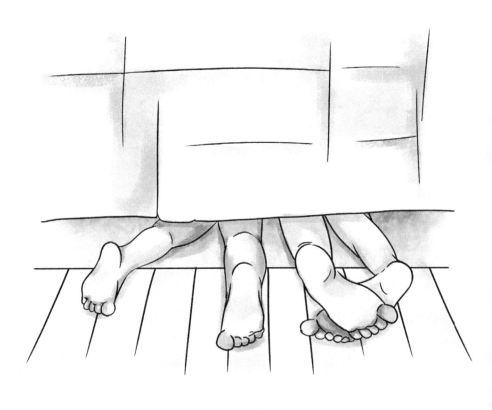

Crow 2

Luis, Luisita and the Luisitos

"Luisa, do you have all your parts?"

"I think so. Are you still here?"

"Where do you think I'd go? This room is very small, and the dizziness is very great."

"You never lose your sense of humor," she said, laughing. "Not even if you're all screwed up. That's why I chose you. Tell me, what are you thinking of doing?"

"I'm not thinking. I'm just sensing the light. I don't know where it comes from, maybe from beneath the door that's still standing. And I don't know where the spilled vodka is, or is it you who smells like it? Everything is very dark outside. It must be nighttime already and... Sorry, what did you say? You chose me?"

"At night? I don't think so. We haven't talked so much since you asked me what the fee was and I told you that if you brought your own weed, it was cheaper, and yes, I chose you. Of course, what kind of work do you do?"

"Shit! The bed frame is dry from licking it so much. I'm thirsty, and there's not a drop left. At least my leg doesn't hurt so badly... I think it's fallen asleep on me or maybe I lost it from being locked up."

"Ouch! My head hurts, too. Maybe on account of so much cheap vodka, the kind you like. Thank God everything fell down on us when we were totally drunk. Die hammered, die happy. Die with the prostitute who chose me. And why do you want to know what kind of work I do? Does being a doctor or a trucker really matter now? Since when does a prostitute care about her client's job?"

19

"Stop calling me that, because I call you by your name and I don't call you an amoral brothel runner. And since we're buried in here, at the very least, I'd rather not die next to a stranger. Well, actually I'm afraid of falling asleep and not waking up again, but if I do and you manage to get out of here, tell my kids I fought to the end. Can you pick something up?"

"We're not going to get out of here; stop insisting. I can't even raise my arms. I didn't hear it coming because you started to move like a broken blender. Everything was spinning, and the lights were all different colors. We don't even know if they're looking for us. Let's hope not. I don't want my kids to know what I was doing with you. I don't give a damn about my wife, but I do care about my kids. They really do matter to me."

"Oh, excuse me! The family man is speaking. The self-sacrificing man who hates his wife but cares what his kids think about him. What are their names? Do they know you hang around in sleazy bars, that you like sex with clowns and being tied up from behind?"

"For God's sake, woman! Luis Manuel is eight, and Luis Fernando is four. And since we're building a friendship of dying brothel fans, have you got a family?"

"Yes. This whore, as you call her, has a family. My daughter, Luisa Sofía, is fourteen, and Luisa Fernanda, the oldest, is sixteen. Their father left us because he didn't want to take care of a whore's daughters. We only fuck occasionally when he has the money to pay me."

"I'm hungry. Stretch out your hand and grab me down here."

"Are you crazy? I can hardly move. Besides, your session expired when you draped yourself over the chandelier so I could lick your crotch."

"The heartless hooker is going to charge me, even on her deathbed?"

"Of course. What if we were to get out of here and you hadn't paid me?"

"And if we don't get out and this is the last dick you have a chance to grab?"

"What if I stick my hand in and your member isn't there?"

"Please, woman! I would've bled out already. And you, are you sure you're all there?"

"No, but at least I don't want to find out and die in anguish."

"Go on, girl, stick your hand in and die happy."

"Luis, don't you understand that I can't move? I've got a lot of weight on my right forearm."

"Of course. All this was an earthquake? Lucky, this room is only one story and is made of wood."

"It shook very hard. Maybe the roof caved in. I'm going to shout."

"No, don't do that! They must be looking for us out there. I don't want them to find me with you like this."

"Do you want to die, then? Go die alone! Help! I'm here! Help!"

"Listen to me! If you start screaming again, I'll put an end to your miserable life, you cheap hooker. I don't want to come out in the papers as the father of the Luisitos who fulfills his obligation but gets drunk with hookers in any old dump."

"Yeah? And how is the wounded gentleman going to do that? By farting? Help! Help!"

"Are you really so drunk and high? I told you not to mix your poisons."

"I hardly drank anything and getting high is an art that only we fine ladies can handle. Besides, what do you care if I got drunk or not? Help! Help!"

"Shut up, Luisa, and let's get out from under the bed; we're gonna wake the kids."

Crow 3

Rot in Hell, Ramón!

Even without a suspicion of death, there had been many books lying open on that afternoon in the library. The next day's imminent exam settled on my neck with the insistence of a bladeless knife. Industrial costs had become out of reach for my purposes, and I didn't want to miss my last chance to pass a class that would let me end the year successfully.

I checked my watch and noticed that something wasn't right.

"Shit, it's 5:00 PM!" I shouted between clenched teeth. Almost at the same moment, the library assistant fixed himself on my recklessness.

"Quiet, please!"

I picked up my things hurriedly and shoved them into my backpack. A bottle of soda that I hadn't managed to throw into the recycle bin ended up at the bottom with my books. Without wasting another second, I ran down the halls of the College of Engineering to catch the only means of transportation available to take me home that day.

Or so I thought.

It was Wednesday afternoon, February 15, 2006, a day when I would log in nearly twenty-four hours without sleep. I lived about forty kilometers away, in the northeastern part of the state, a distance nearly impossible to cover on foot for such a tired body. My friend, Virgilio, had left several messages on my old phone, which I hadn't been able to answer because I had been at the library.

I wonder what that lunatic is up to, I thought, placing the phone in the front right pocket of my jeans, the fabric worn down by the stiffness of the narrow desks.

Virgilio was an average-sized guy with a strange gait and very weighty ideas. I had known him since elementary school. We had shared classrooms and girlfriends, too. Although he had decided not to attend the same college as me, his lifelong dream had been to buy a big, black van, the kind with lots of traction and hardly any silence. He worked hard, and in the end, we celebrated his achievement for almost three days straight. But it wasn't all fun and games.

We also had some vigorous arguments due to his uncontrolled recklessness.

Who else would have the crazy idea of snipping off the seatbelt of his van just because it annoyed him when he drove?

"We've gotta die of something!" he replied, grumbling, as he mutilated the seatbelt from all directions.

There was no way to stop him, because, you see, that's Virgilio for you. The truth is that I had to run a long way to catch up with my ride, which had already left. I remember the bus driver's ironic expression when, even though he'd seen me in his rearview mirror, he pretended not to, and hit the gas with evil intent, distancing me from my only chance to make it home that night.

"Damn you, Ramón, wait for me!" I shouted, throwing everything I had in my hands at him. And everything I had in my hands included an old spiral notebook that I hadn't managed to stuff into my backpack, which landed on the green hull of that bus, disappearing at the on-ramp to the highway. Number ten of a diminished fleet that carried dreams, but also hunger and hands damaged by the rough wood of pencils rebelling against the cruelty of ignorance.

"I missed my ride! This is gonna turn out badly," I thought.

It took me about twenty seconds to catch my breath and straighten my body, though not my morale. I was destroyed.

Without a coin to my name, in my pockets, I carried only the phone and some pencil shavings that I had put there temporarily so I wouldn't have to get up and risk losing my seat at the library. I stumbled around, undone, taking about thirty steps toward an asphalt slope that projected from the roadway. I sat down to try to come to a decision about the long night that awaited me. I needed to get some rest before the exam.

"Rot in hell, Ramón," I shouted helplessly, closing my eyes to think.

When I awoke, I realized I was still sitting up. An hour had gone by. Now, the insolent rain made me understand in no uncertain terms that it didn't want me there anymore. I weighed the possibility of spending the night at the test site, School Auditorium Number 5, which was air-conditioned. I needed to make sure I was wide awake early tomorrow morning. Besides, I knew Fernando, the night watchman there, and his dog Pintas, better known as "Pintas the Mango-Eater." It was quite an experience to hear him bark with joy in the presence of that tropical fruit.

I picked up my backpack and placed it on my head in a useless attempt to protect myself from the now intensive downpour, and I stood to walk toward the building. Just as I started to cross the street, some incandescent headlights came toward me at full speed. "It must be the police," I thought, startled. Around that time, protests on campus had intensified, and the authorities had decided to carry out nighttime patrols to avoid crowds that might lead to new protests, since they were incited by violent political factions. I tried to remain still until the patrol car came closer, to avoid raising false suspicions. However, as soon as the vehicle stopped in front of me, the backpack, which I clumsily gripped in my wet hands, opened, spilling a few items, including the empty soda bottle.

I was in serious trouble.

These bottles were used by violent protestors to build the famous Molotov cocktails that are thrown at police cruisers to make them back off. It seemed like I would find a place in which to spend the night after all, as well as an excuse for missing my exam: a cold cell in Detachment Two, where I would spend no fewer than seventy-two hours while investigations were carried out.

Just what I needed to put the finishing touches on my already screwed-up night!

I confess that the only thing I managed to think was still, "Rot in hell, Ramón!"

The vehicle slowed down.

It approached me like a hunter who knows he's trapped his prey. I stealthily tried to push the bottle fragments aside with my foot so that the police wouldn't see them or blame me for even more wrongdoing. Nerves and fatigue can create a lot of situations that generally work against us.

The vehicle came to a halt. The headlights grew brighter.

I tried to cover my eyes with my forearm, turned my head aside, and wrinkled my brow as hard as I could to avoid the oppressive glow.

Then, I saw a person open the car door and call out:

"Yo, motherfucker!"

A maternally directed slur had never before brought me so much relief. It was Virgilio! Such was the depth of our affection for one another.

I ran like a lost child who's reunited with a mother, and I hugged him and kissed him on the forehead. That lunatic, without knowing it, had come to my rescue.

I wouldn't spend the night with a sodden backpack, or in Auditorium 5 with Pintas, or in a cell with some random thug, or in bed with Ramón's wife. I would go back home, take a warm shower, grab something to eat, and rest in my own bed.

Whenever someone asks me what luck means to me, I tell them about Virgilio.

Once we were in the van, Virgilio remarked that he had been very worried because I didn't answer his calls. I told him I had spent long hours in the library and that I couldn't answer calls there. Then, I told him about that bastard, Ramón.

"We'll have to teach that dickhead a lesson!" he replied, excitedly.

Well, yeah. I couldn't disagree.

For the time being, I just chatted with my friend, since we had forty kilometers ahead of us to ramble on about women, Barcelona's latest soccer match, or the beach vacation we'd planned. All of this, mixed with twenty thousand prayers of thanks.

Virgilio told me that he'd spent the whole day working on his van because something was wrong with it.

"It's a weird little noise. Do you hear it?"

"No. Probably the belt needs changing."

He asked me to put in a CD by our all-time favorite band—my birthday gift to him. I hurried to look for it but couldn't find it.

"Where's the CD?"

"Look for it under the seat."

"It's not here, asshole. Who could've taken it?"

Laughing his head off, he said, "It doesn't matter. I played it when I was fixing the van this morning. It must be under my seat!"

"Don't bend down. You're driving and it's raining."

But, you see, that's Virgilio for you.

He bent down while I tried to hold the steering wheel from my co-pilot's seat.

Suddenly, a boom in the front right portion of the van shook us from side to side. A tire had exploded, and the van started to spin and turn, partly on account of the damp pavement and partly because that's Virgilio for you.

I tried to grab onto anything I could. In just a fraction of a second, I saw a film of my life that ended with a hearty, "Rot in hell, Ramón!"

Virgilio had cut the seatbelt, and consequently I flew through the air and then through the windshield. I fell out onto the road, smashing my head against the guard rail. Everything went dark.

I struggled mightily to stay inside my body on the damp asphalt, but I felt that the rain would shoot me up to the heavens with infinite force.

A taxi driver behind us stopped to keep the other vehicles from running over me. All I could do was raise my hand as a sign that I was still lying there. Blood was everywhere.

My backpack: lost. My exam: missed. My friend was somewhere on or off the highway. My life was about to leave me, just as that ramshackle bus I had tried to catch earlier with all my might.

Some things just can't be avoided, and death is one of the more popular of these, a cliché of abandoned stories. And yet, lying on the asphalt hopelessly made me understand that yes, my life is probably over, but my story will not be forgotten like a blown tire tread, and neither will my friendship with Virgilio.

Much can be said about human foolishness and much, too, about the values life teaches us. That's why, in my final moments, I asked to be allowed to awaken and say goodbye to my family. My friends. My dreams. There was nothing to hope for but a miracle.

My body no longer belonged to me, and the light at the end of the tunnel began to appear, a dazzling light that burned my eyes and splintered them into a thousand pieces.

But what does a pair of broken eyes matter if life is already breaking into crumbs? Even so, I closed them with all my might, until I heard a loud voice above my head. "What are you doing here, Sir?"

Suddenly, I woke up and saw the bright light of a police car bathing me in intense bursts of blue and red. I was still sitting on the asphalt slope that life had decided to bestow upon me, after that bus left me behind to curse Ramón so many times.

Several hours went by, and now, after I told them what had happened, the police would take me home, soaked, to be reunited with my family.

Was it a miracle or a chance to say goodbye? I don't know.

The confusion of having endured such a nightmare inspired me to take my phone out of my pocket to tell Virgilio what a crazy dream I had. A woman picked up on the other end.

"Hello? Good evening."

That bandit is up to one of his tricks, I thought.

"I'm calling for Virgilio, but don't worry. I'll call back later," I said to the elegant female voice.

"Are you a relative of Virgilio's?" asked the sexy voice.

"Yes, I'm his brother," I replied.

"Señor Virgilio had an accident in his van. Apparently, a tire blew, and his vehicle turned over on the highway. I'm talking to you from Central Hospital, where he died. I'm sorry to deliver the bad news like this…"

And just at that moment, the phone fell from my hands, like the last hopes of that night. Again, I felt as if my soul was being torn from me, because in life, we can try to die several times before we're really dead.

Everything began or ended that night. It's hard to know. But there are two things of which I'm sure: One, that death is not definitive, and two, that someday Ramón will rot in hell.

Crow 4

The Legend of the Astronarda

Who could have imagined that the captain's great legacy would turn into something inexplicable?

A dot in a sea of dots. That should have been the answer some people were waiting for.

But the fact was, that even though his arrogance condemned him to reside forever in the dungeons of oblivion, the captain had a real concept of humility that escaped the logic of any inexperienced sailor. Neither from the lips of his own crew, nor through the lenses of passing spyglasses. That would be like overflowing the limits of precision and exactness, something his exhausted sense of opportunity would not forgive.

But really, how many things can be precise or exact in a world that changes every day?

How many things can be precise or exact in a universe whose limits we don't know?

How many things can be precise or exact in this jumble of relative morality?

How many things can be precise or exact in a sea that whimsically decides the future of the vessels sailing from the Iron Peninsula?

From port to starboard, dancing to the rhythm of the crashing waves of the storm, that decision made in August of the year 486 led the captain to cease being who he was, since both truth and the sea have the universal power to transform the life of a sailor. In this way, the rudder can move in an eternal flow of half-truths and infinite seas. The scent of salty wood, bands of rusty iron, and spilled beer, made everyone wonder,

"Who was the captain?" in a manner appropriate to the epic style of those peninsular bars.

And that reply seemed very easy to choose, as long as the captain was a castaway of his own convictions.

Having been born with the clear ambition of sailing the lost waters one day led him to execute two of his skippers and an admiral. The massive breadth of his ambition didn't allow him any margin of error. But the contradiction in this became a cause, stuck in the turbulent waters that expel everyone who wants to be better than someone else.

The great ship, *Astronarda,* she of the thousand storms.

The great ship that summoned the children to the dock, as they innocently awaited the launching of their dreams, witnessed, on that tense August day, the mutiny that pushed the captain toward the shores of some random, forgotten island, a consequence of the rebel sea that will never have real worth for those blinded by Muff the Pirate's treasure.

The crew had decided to put an end to that ridiculous business, which would carry the *Astronarda* to the bottom of the deep, blue sea, surely dragging them along with her. From the bay to the edge of the first cannon, Vice Admiral Vint, the captain's faithful friend, shouted, "Jump now, Captain!"

And even though the score of his life had always been written on the pedestal of the endless fight, the captain's dignity was trapped by his fear of being executed without the right to a pardon by those rough hands, their knuckles corroded by extinguished candles and splinters from the *Astronarda's* ancient masts. And yet, situations like these were the common denominator of many of the tales of the high seas on the Iron Peninsula. The only difference was that, like what happened on that sea, agitated by the euphoria of those August sailors with their rolled-up sleeves, fear also taught the captain to become a castaway on his own vessel.

For the captain and for the *Astronarda,* never again will it be a question of Muff the Pirate's treasure, nor of what will remain in the collective memory of the peninsula, but rather what they will be capable of becoming from now on, thanks to the rebellion of those hard-working sailors.

Crow 5

The Mystery of the Bear's Claw

I

Such simplicity can make you die of fright. Chance occurrences, most of them unexpected. To die of boredom, though, you need complication. Jeff was killed by destiny. Plain and simple. With no extravagances. The typical guy who walks along, hiding his footsteps so he can go unnoticed by other pedestrians.

Jeff Damon Miller seemed to have no goals in life other than to move around unfettered through the streets of Tredstone. Poet, Bohemian, introvert. Everyone recognized him by his gait: head bowed, directionless, with no noticeable details to call attention to his unremarkable way of walking. He just moved along with clumsy, but efficient, stealth to his destination: the next street. With a style that detracted from the conventionality of ordinary walkers, whenever he was obliged to greet someone, he did so with a quick flick of his right hand, which, unlike his gaze, plunged into who-knows-what sort of thoughts, then rose in a symbol of recognition. Big cities are like that. Beyond the enormous buildings' arrogant efforts to hide whatever is going on in their streets, these picturesque, hobble-footed strollers embed themselves in a certain point in our lives. Scenes, one after another, are nailed to the memories of these places.

Life is what one remembers about it, and it would seem almost inappropriate to evoke images of Parque Wolks in 1982, with all its breathable air in the commotion that was Tredstone without pointing out Jeff Miller's brown leather beret and his inevitable foot-tapping, both of them signs of a mild-mannered man of moderate habits. Indifferent to the social bustle of the suburbs, with their political correctness on display, the wanderer in the beret, as everyone knew him, never revealed in any aspect of his behavior the desire to be labeled a "community altruist," someone who wants to know everything. He just walked. That was all we needed to know about him. No one ever saw him arrive anywhere. No one ever heard him say goodbye to confirm their half-formed theories about him.

At the risk of being interrogated by the police, those of us who had seen him for the last time before Christmas knew that, beneath the polyester overcoat discovered in a dumpster at the Parque Wolks Zoo, a man with no apparent interest in crossing paths with death took his pleasure—and even less of an interest—in that event that took place under slightly irregular and attention-grabbing circumstances.

It was a Sunday night when this girl saw his entrails and other, no less scandalous, parts of his body. Without a doubt, my suspicions, as well as those of the other shopkeepers from the neighborhood businesses, were sufficient to eliminate all doubts of their desire not to be seen, though many people still can't help but wonder about the mysterious darkness that covered his pooled blood next to a trash container. On the one hand, the official version is far from likely. On the other, those who think it was a crime committed in cold blood don't know the motives that led him to that situation. What I am sure of is that those who jumped to these quick conclusions had no opportunity to explore the gaps in his complicated personality.

On one occasion, that chubby visitor stopped by the café. An ordinary day in October. Because it might have been any day. A day when his unseemly black shoes—the kind whose worn tips curve comically upward—hesitated at the concrete entryway, and—no longer worried about showing up with his developing baldness sheltered beneath the strange beret—he ordered a sugarless vanilla latte with a sprinkle of cinnamon. Nothing strange about that. Everyone orders a latte at the Rinaldi Coffee Shop. Those who don't usually walk away with regrets. For those skeptical observers, I've got some prefab conversations that allude to the aged photos on the caked plaster wall, which explain the family origin of a café with a long history and a negligible reputation. It's as if bitter justice had straddled the depleted remnants of the sense of tradition of these Tredstonian streets.

The fact is nobody attempts to remember a place like this without something that will make them feel distinguished. In such cases, factors like experience, luxury, and presumption are overlaid. My café's no Starbucks. I don't have enough capital to remodel it. Or rather, I do have the capital, but I don't want to sell illusions. I just sell coffee.

Of course, my Italian grandparents would vehemently protest my self-interested attempts to credit a latte with a fame it doesn't deserve. That distinction should belong to espresso, flying the flag of true Neapolitan customs. However, in a world where the Gardens restaurant turns out to be a hypocritically valid option for representing Italian culinary traditions, my financial convenience percolates in ways that might be called, at the very least, inoffensive. Because I couldn't charge $3.50 for an espresso. That would mean a two-dollar profit for a little milk and caramel. And a pinch of salt. That's the secret. Vanilla doesn't do anything but hike up the price.

With an understanding based on simple observation about his visits, I can be sure that Jeff Miller had never tried either one. That's why I found myself so thoroughly surprised when I saw him show up underneath the black canopy at the entrance to the café, desirous of ordering something for himself. From his intensive, frequent glances in my direction, I suspected a certain attraction toward me. I can't deny that at some point, I finally attributed his usual strolls to a supposed line of rubberneckers outside the café. I also noticed how John Bertolotti, the usual waiter, disliked the now-unfortunate man's rounds. More than once, I noticed how John would go outside to confront him on the street, just to control the introverted passerby's timid stares. John's a good guy. But I know how he feels about me. It's not so bad to feel like the object of desire of two men. However, I'm the owner of this café, and I understand that I'm not the Italian beauty that this strange situation makes me feel like

I am. Maybe the situation seems more like a good opportunity to look into my family history a little. We Rinaldis are recognized in Tredstone as a family of means, but we prefer to maintain the low profile of our traditional values.

As I noticed the disdain with which John took his order, I signaled him to let me wait on him in person. Motivated by curiosity, I headed for the coffee bar. It was the first time I had ever heard his harsh voice, typical of habitual smokers. He uttered phrases in a classic Southern accent of the *y'all* type, which ultimately seemed to drown in unexpected whistles. I suspected Tennessee origins, or possibly Kentucky. He expressed his timidity in small requests for permission to express himself freely. And yet, that display of exaggerated politeness was put aside when he repeated his request. I knew quite well what was coming.

"What can I get for you, Sir?"

"I ordered a latte. Vanilla. A little cinnamon; no sugar. In a to-go cup," he replied confidently, without raising his eyes from the floor.

"Would you like a little spice?" I asked, unaware of the involuntary double entendre I had generated.

"No sugar and just a little cinnamon."

"Got it. Excuse my boldness, but I've often noticed you walking around the neighborhood. Do you live nearby?"

He didn't answer. He didn't look up. He just nodded.

"May I get you anything else? I highly recommend our carrot cake…"

"No, miss. I'm not interested in anything else."

"Katty. Katty Rinaldi."

He nodded again.

After trying to pay the $3.50 bill with a semi-destroyed debit card, I read his name: Jeff D. Miller, embossed on the plastic, worn out by time and misuse. A card that explained by its mere existence the number of closed doors to which he had been spontaneously exposed.

"Okay, Jeff D. That's $3.50."

"Damon…"

"Excuse me?"

"Jeff Damon. That's my name."

"Perfect, Damon…"

"It's Jeff Damon, please."

"Sure. So sorry. Tredstonian customs. The system doesn't recognize your card. Shall I try again, or would you rather use another method of payment?"

"It's the only one I have."

"I'm sorry about the hassle, man. But the damn thing doesn't want to be processed. Banks are so weird. They always want to make us go to their headquarters to try to sell us one of their investment packages."

"I guess I won't be taking that latte, then."

"Oh, no! Don't worry about it. You can take it with you and pay tomorrow. I always see you around. I trust you."

"I'm from Florida and I live five blocks from here. Marshall Residences."

"Florida?" I asked, surprised.

"Jacksonville. I moved to Tredstone when I was sixteen. I'm a writer. A poet, to be more precise. Listen, could I sit at one of your tables to write something?"

"Oh! Of course. It would be an honor to have you here, writing. Do you need something? A pencil? Paper?"

"No, thanks. I've got it all here," he replied, extracting from the torn pocket of his overcoat a small, spiral notebook and a pencil consumed by the rigor of his restless hands.

As any mortal might have imagined of a man of such peculiar habits, his choice to sit at the table farthest from the public eye—at the entrance of the hallway leading to the restrooms—was obvious.

After removing his coat and beret, he assumed a posture that was protective of his little notebook, displaying a zeal that hardly corresponded with the apparent real value of his belongings. Hunched over and leaning slightly toward the table, he made it impossible for anyone to visualize the flight of his left hand. Not even John, who became so agitated that I had to go into the kitchen to calm him down.

"He's just a Bohemian," I told him.

"He's occupying a table with a latte he didn't even pay for," grumbled the waiter along with his sour expression.

"Why does that man bother you so much?"

He glowered at me. I felt his shame take control of his throat before he replied.

"I know people of his class. They claim to be poets and only want to get a little bit involved."

"I understand why you defend the café so firmly. I like your loyalty. But, as a waiter, you can't let your prejudices get in the way of giving our clients good service. And it's my duty…"

"Yes, Ms. Katty. Whatever you say." And again, he returned to the cash register.

I couldn't avoid taking him to the office. It wasn't the first time. I'm a widow, and it's not like I have a lot of contact with men. My husband, Paolo, died of cancer when he was thirty-six. That was five years ago. He died young. I died along with him. His family never accepted me. They saw me as a person who didn't fit in with their family history.

A dispute of this type upset me so much that I couldn't get involved in the game of jealousy and macho territoriality. Having sex with me was the only thing that kept John at the café. Somehow, he needed for that to keep happening. A life devoted to business uses up a forty-something woman's daily allotment of adrenaline. A taste that can only be found in recurring fantasies, bathed in the caramel of the latté maker, and caressed by fleeting encounters of his beard scraping my crotch. The game we played under my desk was fun, though it lacked the passion my breasts need.

Then, I declared my heated ritual over and got ready to leave. I ordered John to take his post and to assure me that everything was under control. After checking my appearance in the office mirror, I walked over to the bar, smoothing out my dress, and noticed that we had only three clients, including the untimely writer at the rear table. Lorena was my other server. When there are no clients, she helps me organize the pantry. She started out by working weekends, but little by little, I managed to convince her to work full time. She gets only Sundays off. We all have Sundays off here. One of my family's Christian traditions. And it also turned out to be more expensive for me, but I couldn't have it any other way. John's job was different. That was also why he earned less than Lorena. All of us were comfortable with this dynamic.

Correcting his eloquence, the disturbing visitor had picked up his pencil in a strange way, with a gesture in which all his fingertips converged simultaneously around the graphite. It was strange to watch him grab the pencil that way. Similarly, it was strange, at the very least, to notice that his "latte to go" still stood on the table, untouched. "Who orders a latte to go and leaves it in the café without touching it?" I wondered, baffled.

Around four hours had gone by since he occupied the table, and after ending the conflict between the writer and a few pages torn out of his notebook, he swiped his right hand across his head and stretched his shoulders. Then, he stood, picked up his things, including the cup of coffee, and left, without further ado. However, some traces of his writing remained, forgotten, on the table. Rejects, perhaps, verging on fruitless sketches. Lorena picked them up. She was getting ready to hide the small papers from my sight when I subtly gestured to her to hand them over.

"Lorena, will you give me those papers, please?"

"Yes, Ms. Katty."

"Nonsense by a nobody!" interrupted John, who had been eavesdropping from the kitchen door.

"Don't be so hard on him. It's a carbon copy of a poem," I said, trying to put the pages in some kind of order. "Interesting, and very kind on his part. He called it 'The Loneliness of a Wanderer.' His signature's down here: Jeff Damon Miller. Are those all the pages?"

"Yes, Ms. Katty. This page here was on the floor…"

I turned to look at John. I gave him a half-smile and read aloud:

Joyful of knowing you,
Observer of your eye-catching curves.
Helpless before your beauty.

Needy of the passionate warmth of your kisses.

Intoxicating,
Spectacular lips.

Tenuous proof that
Hope is the only,
Easiest way to deal with what I feel.

Memorizing each corner, where
Upstairs there are
Rumblings of your unique
Deep scented jasmine.
Enchanting scent that unmistakably
Reflects my intention towards you.
Enchanting scent that unmistakably
Reflects my intention towards love.

Jeff Damon Miller

"Hah! Pure garbage," John said, picking up his apron.

"It's very…sensitive…He seems like a very lonely man," I responded to John's silence.

In what I recognized as a notable habit, and despite the fact that he passed our street every day at 3:15 PM, he never again stopped by at the café. From inside, I greeted him—"Hi, Jeff!"—to which he managed to respond with his customary gesture. In my mind, I kept a couple of stanzas of his poem, which I tried to use as an irreverent excuse for carrying on a conversation with that strange character. I can't deny that I thought my latte hadn't been good enough to convince him to settle his debt and become a regular customer, or that I had somehow annoyed him with my conversation. Later, I assumed that the man had always intended to pay with his poetry.

Even later, both Linda, the owner of Linda's Laundry, and George, the old grouch from the corner drugstore, assured me that they had seen him at their shops one time only. In George's case, it didn't exactly shock me. Not too many people bond with the owner of a drugstore called Iain old *Pharmacy*. That's what he was like. A man of few (or no) words, with breath that reeked of Jack Daniels, who easily revealed the solitary habits of a hard-core drinker. To my credit and in honor of the good fortune I believed I'd had that October afternoon, I deduced that I was the only person with whom Jeff exchanged a few friendly gestures, which made me even more convinced of my romantic suppositions.

However, a couple of weeks after the unfortunate event, the Tredstone papers were still talking about an attack committed by a bear that had escaped from the zoo, assaulted Jeff, and stuffed his innards into his mouth. The bear was never found. The savage butchery was carried out with great viciousness, which gave rise to the most extraordinary theories: that it had been an act of revenge by the Mafia, a debt collected from the wrong person, or a drug cartel incident in which Jeff played the role of an important distributor in the region. His introverted, unfriendly personality even led many people to paint him in disturbing ways: as a pedophile, a rapist, a smuggler—anything and everything, all sorts of signs, which, of course, couldn't be confirmed by the police.

II

Breaking news: We're here with our correspondent, Richard Goodman, at the Parque Wolks Zoo, where apparently, sometime after 9:00 P.M., a young grizzly bear named Tiberius escaped and fatally wounded a man identified as Jeff Damon Miller, age fifty-three. Authorities have not yet confirmed this information, while zoo officials deny the animal's escape.

"Trevor, turn off that crap. Whadda we have?"

"Jeff Damon Miller. Fifty-three years old. From Jacksonville, Florida. Rents an apartment at Marshall Residences, north of the city. Single. The neighbors didn't have much contact with him. We suspect the perp was one of the younger grizzlies in the zoo. We've alerted Animal Welfare."

"At the zoo, they say that Tiberius' cage is empty because last night, he succumbed to lung disease. But no one has come up with any official certification of this. The records aren't public, and according to county protocol, the animal's body was used to feed the big cats. We're trying to verify this information with the mayor's office, but if someone from the local zoo is involved in a cover-up, we're dealing with a killer bear on the loose, or one that was 'disappeared on purpose.'"

"How do you arrive at the conclusion that it might have been a bear? The big cats devoured a four-hundred-fifty-pound bear in a single day?"

"If you examine the abdominal wounds carefully, they appear to have been made by something resembling bear claws. They must have entered from both sides, at an angle that can be achieved only from the rear section. The marks over here—do you see them?—make me think that it held him down from behind and ripped him open. Then, it dragged its kill away. It was much easier to hide behind the shrubs. It attacked and fled. The girl who found the body says she saw a large shadow run very quickly through those shrubs over there."

"A bear that size could take you down with a single paw. And judging from his knees and the palms of his hands, this man doesn't appear to have fallen face down."

"It's possible the bear waited for his opportunity but didn't strike. But we have no witnesses of the attack. These animals are unpredictable. My father was a hunter in Wyoming. You never know what to expect from them, especially when they've been in captivity for so long."

"On the other hand, we've talked to some of the neighbors at the Marshall Residences. They said they saw the victim having a very heated discussion with the person in charge of collecting the rent. It's this guy: Preston J. Benson, age thirty-five, from Oklahoma," said Trevor, showing me a photograph. "Mr. Benson has a record of robbery, illegal transportation of firearms, drug trafficking, and domestic violence."

"A real jewel in the crown…I don't know, Trevor…We need to interrogate this guy. I want to check the security cameras in all the local businesses, buildings, houses, traffic lights. Everything within a two-mile radius. Let's start with the most direct route to the Marshall Residences. What worries me now with regard to a bear is that a beast that size doesn't have too many places to hide. Where's the woman who found him?"

"Ms. Lorena Rasmussen. Waitress, twenty-four years old. She was walking her dog when it detoured into the bushes. She's over there, with the paramedics. She's having a nervous breakdown."

"I don't blame her. I'm having a nervous breakdown."

"We also found this beret next to the body."

"Let the lab examine it. What else do we have?"

"As of now, it's nighttime and the park is closed, but nothing else."

"I don't see any large animal footprints around here. Check out the nearby shrubbery carefully. Maybe we'll find a trace of our teddy bear."

With more doubts than answers, I headed toward the ambulance parked along the side of the road. "A bear…damn it," I thought.

"Ms. Rasmussen, how do you do? I'm Detective Evan McCarthy of the Tredstone Police Department, Homicide Division. Do you have time to answer a few questions?"

"It was awful! All this…" the girl exclaimed between sobs.

"I understand. Did you see anyone suspicious in the park or near the body?"

"It was all very confusing. It's nighttime, but I saw the shadow of something very big behind the bushes. I couldn't make out what it was. It ran off very quickly."

"I see. And do you often go to the park at this time of night?"

"It's because of my dog, Kiki. I take him for a walk. He's five years old. Sunday is my day off. I try to make the most of it."

"Kiki! Strange name for a Rottweiler that size. Ms. Rasmussen, did you know the victim?"

"I didn't recognize him right away in the darkness. But that man was kind of a hippie who once came to the café where I work."

"Rinaldi Coffee Shop, right? And excuse my curiosity, but, you know, we detectives are like that…How could you recognize him so easily if he only stopped by the café once?"

"I don't know… he often walks along the street in front of the café…"

"I see. Ms. Rasmussen and Kiki, right?" I said, staring at that dog's disturbing face. "May I take a saliva sample from your dog's teeth?"

"What are you suggesting, Detective? Kiki would never attack anybody."

"Sorry, Miss. It's just routine procedure. Would you separate your darling pet's jaws, please?" I asked, triggering the laughter of the paramedics and my police department colleagues.

"You could do it yourself. Like I said, Kiki is harmless. But if that's what you want…"

I proceeded to introduce the tube into the canine's mouth to collect the sample.

"A little wider, please," I said, inserting the swab toward the dog's upper jaw.

"Kiki has big teeth. Did he move the body around?"

"No, not at all. I took him away where the bushes begin."

"We're done, Ms. Rasmussen. Here's my card. Please don't hesitate to call in case you remember anything else."

"Thank you, Detective, but I've told you everything I saw."

"Again, it's just routine."

"McCarthy!" shouted Trevor insistently from the place where the body was found. You've gotta see this…"

"What is it?"

"It's something like a note. It was in a hidden pocket of the beret."

"A note? In a hidden compartment? What the hell does it say? Let me read it," I said to Trevor, grabbing that mysterious note with a tweezer and taking advantage of the faint light of an incandescent bulb behind me. My life ends at the beginning of each verse."

"What do you think of this?" Trevor asked, undaunted.

"There's something here that doesn't quite convince me. The note itself can be interpreted in many ways. Something philosophical or who knows what…The man was a Bohemian. But taken all together, it doesn't make much sense to me."

"The girl who found the body was lying. I don't know her reasons, but the dog had traces of blood on its back teeth. She said that the dog didn't go near the victim. Let's give forensics a chance to confirm the animal's tracks on the body."

"C'mon, McCarthy! Do you think the dog killed him?" replied Trevor, obviously confused.

"No. I'm just saying that her story isn't real. Why would she change the facts?"

"She might have been very nervous. In all the confusion, it's possible she forgot."

"Let's see if she's able to stick with her version."

III

"Mr. Preston Benson?"

"Oh, shit."

"We're detectives from the Tredstone Police. Beside me is Detective Trevor Sánchez, and yours truly, who has the honor of being your host today, Detective Evan McCarthy of the Homicide Unit. We're the good guys behind the shit."

"Homicide? What the fuck do you want? I've never killed anybody. Whatever you may think of me is false. I'm not involved in that stuff anymore. I've got a job now, and a family."

"We want to talk to you about this man," I said, showing the nervous guy a photo of the victim's corpse. "Jeff D. Miller. As you no doubt already know, he died a few days ago, and some neighbors said that…"

"Yeah, yeah…that I attacked the motherfucker, even though it was just a couple of shoves. But he had it coming! That crook is—was—a con man!"

I looked at Trevor, confused. Then, I asked, "You also threatened to kill him, didn't you? Besides, what does the distinguished Mr. Benson base his accusation on?"

"Look, detective, that piece of shit tried to pay his last month's rent with a gold chain, which I accepted to help him out. You know, he would've ended up in the street if I had told the landlord he was behind in his rent. It wasn't the first time he was late. The chain turned out to be phony. I was in trouble and nearly lost my job over that. And there isn't exactly an oversupply of jobs for people with a record like mine…"

"And for that, he deserved to die? Mr. Benson, could you tell us where you were on the night of December 26?"

"Dammit, Detective! I was in Cleveland, with my family. We spent Christmas night with my wife's father, and we got here on the 28th, just after 6:00 PM."

"Have you got anything to confirm your alibi?"

"For fuck's sake! You're the cops. You go find out."

"We could do it, but with you behind bars. Let me remind you that you attacked and threatened a murder victim."

"Well…well…Shit! Okay, wait…Here it is, in my wallet. It's a receipt from a gas station. See it? That day I was in Cleveland! It says so clearly, right here: water, cigarettes, condoms…"

"We could check it out later with the cameras at the gas station," I said, turning to look at Trevor. "Now, my honorable Mr. Benton, may we see the chain?"

"That piece of crap? Yeah, sure! Here it is! The locket is real gold. Not eighteen karats, but…well, the chain isn't."

"Oh, interesting. Did Mr. Miller tell you what this chain meant to him? I'm referring to these initials here, on the clasp: 'P.R.'"

"No. Not at all. I'm not interested in the dark side of other people's lives. Now, my unwanted detectives, if you've finished…"

"Wait! What a rude way to treat visitors!" I said to Benson, grabbing the door before it slammed. "Did you say, 'the dark side of other people's lives'?"

"That guy was strange. My wife is in charge of cleaning the apartments. One day, she picked up some bags with wigs from his trash can, along with women's underwear, chains, and other crazy stuff…"

"Did anyone visit him frequently? Some stranger—I mean, someone who stood out?"

"Detective, that's a very round-about way of asking if drag queens came to visit him."

"I didn't say that."

"The answer is yes. In fact, one day, from the building hallway, I saw him drunk, closing the door, and wearing a very flashy outfit. He was with a couple of drag queens I had never seen in my life. Very ugly, that's for sure…"

"I see. Did you know, Mr. Benson, that this locket opens up?" I asked, carefully removing the cover.

"Well, no. I didn't touch this piece of junk until you guys showed up to interrupt my lunch."

Once the little gold locket had been opened, our astonishment was, at the very least, perplexing.

IV

On entering Jeff D. Miller's apartment on the third floor of the Marshall Residences, I was able to confirm the careless, Bohemian nature of that ill-fated man. It was a very grubby hole in the wall that smelled strongly of humidity. It consisted of one small room, like a studio, about two hundred fifty square feet. To the right, and in front of the only window that looked out onto the parking lot, was an iron cot in a very sorry state, reinforced with pieces of cardboard. A pigsty.

Trevor and I divided the work. He went to interrogate the manager of the zoo, and I decided to take a stroll through the apartment of the strange Jeff D. Miller.

"Oh, yeah!" I exclaimed as I opened the door of the only wardrobe in the apartment. Hardly any clothes, and lots of wigs. "This dude really knew how to party," I thought.

I tripped over some cans lying on the floor. A few roaches scurried off when I closed the wardrobe door. On the back wall, I noticed a poster in very bad condition: 'Borges in Italy,' was written on the lower left. Beneath that, a hasty signature, written by hand in blue ink, read, 'I'll never forget you. P.R.'

"I have to find out who in the hell P.R. is," I said dubiously.

Beside the bed was a very large box. All sorts of books were inside: poetry, novels, essays—everything. Classical literature, very damaged, ravaged by moths. The books revealed random marks. It was clear that Jeff had been a very seasoned reader. Underneath the soiled sheets, I found a notebook, its cover dried out by the sun and gouged by the sweat of the hands that had usually held it. From what I could determine, it was a diary. *Voilà! This is what I was looking for*, I thought.

I was interested in finding some reference to the initials 'P.R.', or to the revealing image inside Benson's locket, or to the note that was found in the beret on the day he died. Some clue that might lead us to Jeff's real killer. It was clear that it hadn't been a bear.

Let's see. What have we got here? I wondered. Brief quotes on page one, a few phrases jotted down—randomly it seems—on all the pages. Addresses, phone numbers...Suddenly the association with the initials of those names made sense. Jackson Hoffman. No, couldn't it be J.H. Miranda Sandberg, Victor Rintasky, Aron Fawler, shit! They're not in alphabetical order. Here it is! But it shows up as P.R. and has no phone number associated with it!

On the other hand, those footnotes referring to the initials powerfully called my attention:

> *Without you I am a wanderer, a poor writer with his own pains.*
> *My Italian treasure with the aroma of coffee.*

As I turned the page, some small sheets of paper fell to the floor. I bent down to pick them up, since one of them had landed under the bed. After pushing aside some old shoes and other impediments, I gave them a closer look. It seemed to be a poem signed by Jeff Damon Miller: 'The Loneliness of a Wanderer.' Inside the notebook, I also found a carefully folded napkin. When I removed it from the notebook, I could see coffee stains. *What's this?* I asked myself, confused. The logo read: 'Rinaldi Coffee Shop.'

"And isn't this the café where the witness who found the body worked?" I wondered.

At the same time, I heard the door handle move behind me. Someone was trying to break into the room.

"Who's there?" I asked.

I heard footsteps moving very quickly, outside, in the hall. I let go of the notebook and drew my weapon. I left immediately, trying to see something in between the flickering of the fluorescent tubes on the ceiling, almost invisible. About four meters from where I stood, a shadow hurried downstairs. Judging from the sound of the footsteps, it was a large individual.

"Halt! Police!"

I ran down the stairs, trying to reach the first floor. I accidentally hit my shoulder against a fire extinguisher that had been badly hung on the wall. My service weapon fell next to the door that led to the parking lot. Outside, I heard a car motor revving up. I tried to pick up my weapon and get out of there. Three shots were fired at the wall. To avoid the bullets, I threw myself on the floor next to the weapon. The car came closer. The gunshots ended. Weapon in hand, I opened the door in time to see a black van—an older model—fleeing. I ran to my car, about ten meters away. I couldn't do anything: it had gotten away. I picked up the radio and requested units to follow a black van down Birmingham Street.

I immediately decided to go upstairs to Jeff's room to collect the diary and take it to headquarters. However, someone had taken advantage of the chase to enter the apartment and take it.

They had also ripped the 'Borges in Italy' poster from the wall.

There was an image in red spray paint, similar to the one found in the gold locket that I had turned over to Benson. It was a bear claw inside an inverted triangle. They even had had the nerve to sign it to confirm our suspicions. They were mocking us. They signed it with two initials: P.R.

V

"The note in the beret, the poem in the notebook…this man knew his life was in danger," said Trevor, astonished.

"There's a copy."

"What are you saying?"

"There's a copy of the poem in the notebook. I saw the pieces of carbon paper before the attack. Have you found any reference to the symbol with the golden claws?"

"No. It must be a secret society or something like that…For some shamans, bear claws symbolize strength, courage, defense, protection…"

"Shamans," I said, confused. "What do you know about the café? Do we have a search warrant from the judge?"

"It's in the name of a certain individual. We haven't been able to find out much about him. A certain John Bertolotti. He lives on Browers, number seventy-five. And yes, the warrant arrived this morning. Although Judge Robson wasn't very convinced. The bear story left us a little off base… I had to move a few contacts and collect a few favors."

"And what role does Katty Rinaldi play in all this?"

"No idea, McCarthy."

"She has the same last name as the café, and yet the owner is the waiter. On the other hand, what could've caused those wounds on Jeff?"

"Pliers?"

"Or a sharpened hand like Freddy Krueger's? We need to visit his friends at the café. And we need to do it now. It's strange, at the very least, that a café called Rinaldi Coffee Shop should have as its only owner a man called Bertolotti, with an uneventful life. I think, my dear Trevor, that we're getting closer to the bottom of this."

"What about the poem in the notebook? Do you remember anything?"

"Just that the title is 'The Loneliness of a Wanderer.' And it's sort of like a heartbreaking tale of romantic rejection."

Then, Trevor and I picked up our overcoats and, after exploring the whole city, including Parque Wolks, we arrived at the café. Oddly, it was closed, and it was Monday. We decided to enter through the back door, the one that had direct access to the kitchen. A few agents were outside, checking the garbage can. Trevor, as well as a couple of agents and I forced the entrance open after making sure no one would open the door on us from the other side.

"It's all clear!" the agents said after making sure we wouldn't have an unpleasant encounter.

I ordered the agents to concentrate on the room where the pantry was located. Trevor would do the same in the kitchen. I wanted to investigate the little office.

"Something smells awful in here!"

"Trevor!" I yelled immediately.

I opened the office door and turned on the light.

Lorena Rasmussen was there, her throat slit. Beside her, the Rottweiler, Kiki, was the same.

"Damn! We got here too late!" I said to Trevor as we left the café. "I want you all to check this site from top to bottom!" I shouted, enraged.

"Where are you going, McCarthy?" Trevor asked, coming out to meet me.

"I'm going to look for that motherfucker. Did you see the plant in the office?"

"No."

"It's a bear claw. In the towns of the Sierra de Gredos, in Spain, there's a legend that someone made an offering to God some four hundred years ago at the entrance of the church of Saint John the Baptist, as a gesture of thanks for being saved from a bear attack. The townspeople refuse to change the doors."

"And what's that supposed to mean?"

"The stranger killed the bear. He did it with a scythe. John Bertolotti isn't Italian; he's Spanish, the son of Italian immigrants. Somebody owes his life to somebody else at that café. The plant in the office and the symbolism of the bear represent…"

"Gratitude!" exclaimed Trevor.

"Detectives!" yelled one of the agents, emerging from the café.

"What do we have?" I replied, about to climb into the car.

"These are the copies of the poem…"

"Excellent discovery! Let me see them," I demanded, collecting the copies. "Keep looking. We're on the trail of a possible murder weapon, or at least, a scythe."

"At last, we can check the poem to decipher the riddle of the note in the beret," replied Trevor, excitedly.

"Here it is!" I yelled, poking the pages with my index finger. "That Jeff Miller was a genius! Look at the words that are formed with the first letter of each line of the poem."

"J, o, h, n. John is the murderer. But what about P.R., the initials?"

"You're about to find out, my friend. First, we have to find those lowlifes John Bertolotti and…Paolo Rinaldi."

"Paolo Rinaldi?"

"Katty…isn't a she, my dear Trevor. She was a man before her sex change. Paolo Rinaldi was Jeff Miller's romantic partner. Her family was opposed to her changes, and she had to be admitted to a psychiatric hospital because of the emotional shock. She doesn't remember much about her past, which is why she turned the café, the only property she owned, over to John's name.

"They literally saved each other's lives. They hired Lorena Rasmussen because she was blackmailing them; otherwise, she wouldn't have earned so much as an assistant. They used her that night in the park as a lookout, to make sure no one was nearby, while John attacked Jeff from behind."

"The day they attacked me, Paolo Rinaldi went to Jeff's house to get rid of everything with his initials on it. That's why they took the poster of 'Borges in Italy.' And the notebook."

"Excellent work, McCarthy!"

"They murdered him in the park, before trying to make us believe it had been a bear. They paid the caretaker at the zoo to kill the animal and make it disappear the night before."

"And how do you know that?"

"Here's the evidence…The caretaker received a money order for fifty thousand dollars from an account in Spain in the name of John Bertolotti."

After demonstrating that they had abandoned their houses and, additionally, had bought themselves airline tickets for Russia, the detectives managed to detain John Lucas Bertolotti and Paolo Gabrielle Rinaldi at the airport.

One year later, the murderous couple was sentenced to fifty years in Tredstone State Prison. The scythes were never found.

Crow 6

Madame Lingerie

I learned that life is one thing, and reality is quite another. You can wait around for life, but reality is right in front of you all the time, whether you like it or not.

Like the double pair of twos I threw in a dice game, unwanted. I needed a four and a six. It was a ladder. Sex any way I want it, for ten minutes. There's no six in that combination, but ten minutes are enough. For Ernesto, however, I'll have life, and he'll have his reality. A pair of ones, two threes, and a five. For the twos and threes, he wins a kiss down there. He'll have to take Diva Blue or Bloody Mary. Two stars. If she likes him, she might give him something more, but it's not a sure thing. Ernesto's dick is so tiny that when he pees it looks like that Michael Jackson dance step, leaning forward and holding on to the wall.

For a five, though, they'll thank him at the hotel. Ah, and a nice cold one's not so bad, either, though Ernesto gets annoyed. They give that to all of us, while I, in addition to my beer, will get ten minutes of reality with Madame Lingerie. Because that's how things work, and she's the one I want. It's more expensive for a four-star model—three hundred a glass with five dice and two shots. Those are the rules, and he bet one hundred fifty dollars to play twice.

"Whatever's cheaper, that's what I want because you get more for your money." He practices mental poverty. If you can pay the most, don't buy the cheapest, because then the poverty will move from your wallet to your mind, and from there, it'll be hard to get it out. Before, we used to do it his way. Everything arranged to make him feel good. Ernesto isn't one of those guys who live for today because there might be problems tomorrow. Everything is reduced to that: life, reality. He runs slowly away from risks and doesn't like to bet. He's here because he needs to convince himself that he's not overflowing with fear, but rather inspired by precaution. Five dice, but a roll of money that doesn't even belong to him, because it's a little of what Dad had. Just a little. The same thing happened yesterday with the acres of land he left us in Newfoundland. They're worth twice as much as what the buyers are offering, but Ernesto wants to sell because "who knows if there'll be another buyer tomorrow."

I walk over to the phone on the shelf and call Don Fulgencio Arreaza in front of him. We won't sell to him for less than five million. He disappears into his room, with his hotheaded childishness, clicking his heels hard, burying himself in the floor. Later, I'll talk to him, and it'll pass. Life, reality. It's more complicated at night because he likes to sleep on his decisions, discussing dilemmas with his pillow and his Star Wars sheets. Even though he's twenty-five now, he still likes Skywalker and has lightsabers and all sorts of collections around the room. He's different from me. His grandmother raised him after the divorce, but he likes women, at least Diva Blue. He believes the story that she's his girlfriend just because a two-star girl has to be more generous with her limited clientele. She's not bad, but Madame Lingerie…Oh, God! That's heaven with lipstick.

"You've got two ones and two threes. Pay for a recharge and try for a full house with the two or the three."

"A recharge costs three hundred. Are you crazy?"

"Yeah, but you won't lose Diva Blue, and besides, you can win a VIP pass with four stars."

"Next round, gentlemen. Are you in or out?" asks the croupier.

"I'm leaving. I'm going to the roulette wheel," says Ernesto, abashedly. "And I'll look for the three-star throws."

"I'll recharge. With a two." I point to the croupier with one hand as I drink my beer.

"You're crazy, bro."

"Ten chips on two," announces the croupier.

"I want two hours with Madame Lingerie…" I tell Ernesto.

"Do whatever you want. I'm going to the roulette wheel."

"Okay…okay…I know…Let me concentrate on this throw."

I take the cup and rise from my seat. I check the dice; I can't touch them. I watch the croupier, who extends the wand to separate the chips.

I'm throwing for a recharge. And there it goes…A three, a five, a six, and two fours. The house wins.

"Dammit! Not a single two…"

Ernesto isn't completely gone; he's stuck halfway in between so he can watch. I thought he'd stomp hard again. But no; in fact, his face relaxes a little. He lost, but then so did I. Now, he won't be so miserable. Or maybe he will. But at least he'll be miserable in good company.

"Double or nothing!" I shout determinedly and without giving the matter much thought.

"What the hell are you doing, David? Let's go to the roulette wheel," Ernesto interjects from the rear.

"Double or nothing?" the croupier asks. "Twenty chips on two!"

"Yes," I affirm, emboldened and pushing all my chips to the front of the table.

The roulette wheel stops. The waiters crowd behind the croupier to see the spin, but not before placing the open liquor menu in front of me. I can order three free drinks of the highest quality, thanks to my bet. The old guy in the yellow tie who was playing at one end of the table moves toward the left. Behind me, David puts his hands on his head, though first, he stumbles over his beer, spilling it. The slot machines ring out loudly because they're not interested in my madness.

The slots keep going; the jackpot is tougher. With a full house, I could spend the afternoon with Madame Lingerie and enjoy an open bar.

"Double or nothing! And there it goes…Four sixes…"

A resounding shout at the table. The other die is still spinning on one corner, like a diamond turned into a top.

"Sixes! Sixes!" Everyone has their fingers crossed, but the die still doesn't fall.

David grabs me from behind, jumping up and down excitedly.

"Let's go! Let's go! Let's go!" David shouts. "If you win, you can give me the four-star girl..."

The slots quiet down a little to pay attention. I try to drink a beer from a glass that's completely empty. The die falls over. I lost!

Once again, life or reality! I bring my hands to my head. I'm done for. Many don't understand my reaction, though there's also total commotion in the room because it's damn sixes, giving me access to The Damsel or any other premium category for three days at the hotel, all expenses paid.

However, after I manage to command the complete attention of all those present, absolute silence falls on the room.

"I don't want sixes! I'll pay the recharge for twos!" I say, striking the table with both fists. "All I want are my two hours with Madame Lingerie!"

Crow 7

Crow Salad

JUST PLAIN SEVERO

I heard him walk in. He hasn't screamed yet.

I heard him trip over the jars in the living room as he waited for his dinner. He arrived later than usual; no doubt he had been at Dionisio's virtual bar, absorbed in stories of his wanderings so that between each round of beers, his casual friends would celebrate his talent for planting tomatoes in the organoponic farm where he's been working for as long as I can remember.

My brother and I went to bed at seven to avoid his anger and his even louder shouts directed toward our mother. There were two of us boys. Severo Ignacio, age sixteen, was already an adult, and therefore, he had been implanted with a cranial chip. He was the one who was beaten the most. And I, just Severo, was fourteen. Mom told me that those who weren't firstborn didn't need a middle name. My father wanted it that way and didn't allow her to have kids until the Amber License allowed her to give birth to boys only—a situation for which she had to wait four years to achieve.

"Women are kind of useless," he often remarked.

We live on the vast megaplatform of San Carrascal in the year 2139, and although technology and the new global reorganization have brought about great changes for the beings of this planet, there are some things that have not yet changed and that could still get worse.

Now in bed, I pulled my bedclothes over my head in case he opened the door, but the last time he did, it was because he thought I had

63

escaped through the window to play with Alberto, the neighbor's son. My earnings from selling my mom's cupcakes allowed me to buy two LG Max collectible soldiers with their own anti-gravitational megapropellers, which spent more time at Alberto's house than in my hands to keep them out of my dad's sight.

"You damn little brat! Take that sheet off your head so I can see your face!"

"Here I am," I said, pretending to be newly awakened.

"What do you mean 'here I am?' Have you forgotten that I'm your father?"

"Excuse me, Father. I was dreaming and woke up suddenly."

"I'd better not find out that you're hanging out in the street like a bum. First thing tomorrow, I want you in the living room, ready to go to the shed with me. Work is what a real man is supposed to do!"

Severo Ignacio pretended not to hear the conversation unfold.

I had no alarm clock, and besides, I knew I couldn't obey that order. To remain asleep would have meant a beating, not only for me, but also for my mother. That was why, at 4:00 AM, I was already in the living room, dressed in my school clothes and with my backpack ready, waiting for a well-timed change of opinion. My mother watched me from the kitchen, like someone watching a young steer before it's singled out for sacrifice. Sometimes, that man would get up in a good mood and leave us a few Neurocoins for food that day. Other times, we weren't so lucky and had to do our homework at the Plaza del Monumento a Santiago, selling my mom's pumpkin cupcakes on the platform.

We sold them for a quarter Neurocoin apiece; however, they were so good that Ignacio and I raised the price to three for a Neurocoin. Ever since my brother became an adult, we started using his cranial implant to hide our profits and buy fantastic toys that we later hid at Alberto's house. That's how things worked. Before, we used to do all the transactions through my mom's portable bank, which she had secretly acquired with the help of a friend who worked in Amber's commercial sector. But not anymore.

Instead of letting me use the bicycle for three months, Ignacio had convinced me to secretly let him buy a small firearm to practice shooting with. He was very good at it and dreamed of going to the Balastrán Olympics in 2149, representing San Carrascal. He would be the first Carrascaline to compete in the Olympics in Android sharpshooting!

I remember that for the school science fair, he invented a homemade weapon with which he knocked over all the cans from ten meters away. On the other hand, my mother knew what we were up to because several clients had mentioned our price hike to her, but even so, she didn't say anything to us. She just asked us to be at home by five to avoid problems with him. When we got home, we bathed and ate quickly so that we could go to bed before he returned from work. I knew that going off to the hydroponic gardens meant giving up my daily earnings to lug heavy bags of fertilizer and receive severe beatings if any of them happened to tear.

"Life isn't for the weak or for those who make mistakes," my father said. And he whipped me with his thin wire whip, which he always kept tied to his waist with a green cord from the fertilizer bags. One day, I manage to receive eighteen lashes, and I had only dropped two bags, because the other one was already torn on arrival.

"That one was already torn, Father!"

"Useless and a liar!" And he doubled the number of strokes.

When I returned home and saw my mother even more bruised than I was, they put icepacks on my arms and legs to keep the inflammation down and hide the marks a little. The next day, I went to school wearing very loose clothing with long sleeves. The other kids called me "Severo Bartolo," after the comic character, because of my outfit and because I had no middle name.

"Severo Bartolo, shirt like a bag! Severo Bartolo, dressed like a fag!"

"Don't call me that! And leave me alone or I'll tell the teacher!"

"Severo Bartolo, don't wanna play. Severo Bartolo, we all know he's gay!"

I covered my ears and hid in the holographic library. No kid would ever dare go in there of his own free will. But even so, it was better to spend all morning alone among the books, rather than go to the shed to be marked by the wire whip and by his scornful expression.

Yes, that's who I am: just plain Severo.

A full-fledged "implantee," whom life has taught the hard way that it isn't made for weaklings or for those who make mistakes.

The Great Global Community

It's been almost a century since the Great Global Community was founded, when the two last cybernetic emporiums, Holgram and Nex, "fused" and became a single entity, Amber, the power nexus of the Great Global Community. Too bad for Holgram. Their neurotransmitters were always more powerful. But Nex took the lead since the beginning of the World Civil War, which was fought for the independence of human thought on the ancient planet Earth, today rebaptized as the "Great Global Community." Nex succeeded in mandating the installation of cranial chips, which, in just a few weeks, replaced obsolete cell phone communication, so that it might be said that Nex created artificial telepathy to remove Holgram from the competition for cyber control.

Everything changed drastically when the ambitious James Atford, former CEO of Holgram, agreed to sell Nex databases containing the personal information of more than three quarters of the world's population, which unleashed a chain of massive protests that put the global economic system in check. Immediately afterward came the Great Flood, a result of the Greenhouse Effect, and the rest is part of history. As if that weren't enough, the Antarctic thaw revealed the presence of ancient alien bases installed on earth ages ago.

Both the Chinese and North American governments were forced to turn over their political-military power to Nex, which was the only entity on Earth with enough capacity to organize an army of androids to protect the last parcels of terra firma on the planet. That was how the Great Global Community was born, a product of the so-called "International

Reunification Accords," which really were parcels of land auctioned off via Wall Street, and which, in the end, forced the negotiations for the definitive expulsion of the alien race.

Ever since then, and with the help of extraterrestrial technology, the existence of inter-oceanic megaplatforms has allowed for life on the planet despite the ancient continental land masses. The last natural resources, which had been stored by Nex on artificial farms, were relocated to areas restricted by Amber and guarded by armies of androids that had supposedly been created to expel "the alien invasion," which allowed the societies occupying the megaplatforms to develop centers of hydroponic autosustainability, like the one where my father worked. They also control protein production, utilizing wind power, and even the limited generation of oxygen. In short, they control everything.

Meanwhile, we implantees—as humans with a cranial chip are now called—live on megaplatforms built to house groups of people zoned by genetic selection.

The global population is limited in number and gender, which means that to procreate, one has to obtain a license from Amber to unblock the cranial function that stimulates the creation of sperm in men and also "suggests" the genetic characteristics of the human being to be conceived. As one might expect, my father wasn't prepared to foot the cost of advanced conception technology, since, depending on the type of license acquired, it was possible even to choose the hair color of one's descendants, who might even be free of hereditary illnesses or other genetic conditions that were eradicated a long time ago. However, I was born with a basic license that didn't prevent my prominent crossed eyes.

That was my father. The same one who wouldn't let me buy toys, but who, in spite of his defects, was able to forge my character as a responsible man, highly effective in attaining all the goals he sets out for himself.

When I became an adult, I understood that toys weren't necessary. My ridiculous and immature childish whim caused a tragedy that could have been avoided, if I had only gone to that shed to become a real man.

The Fault

At 4:00 AM, I was already in the living room, dressed in my school clothes and with my backpack ready, waiting for a sudden change of plan. At 4:10, my father emerged from his room. His punctuality was remarkable.

As usual, he spanked my mother, who didn't even turn around to face him. The man, fortified by the imminent day's work ahead of him, let loose a yawn and walked toward the living room.

"So, you're planning to carry bags of fertilizer in that shirt?" he asked me, threateningly.

"Father, I have an important test at school today and—"

Without having finished my sentence, I had already earned my first whipping of the day.

"That's enough, Severo!" shouted my mother, who walked in from the kitchen with a large butcher knife in her trembling hand.

"And who the hell do you think you are?" he said to her at the same time he grabbed one of the clay pots that decorated the living room.

I had never seen my mother make an error of that kind. I tried my best to snatch the pot away from him with both hands, but he pushed me so hard that I ended up against the railing of the staircase that led to the upper floor of the house, knocking over the little table with photos that stood alongside it. My mother tried to protect herself behind a long, old-fashioned wooden china cabinet that separated the living room from the kitchen, but the blow to her head was so sharp that I couldn't scream loud enough to avoid hearing the thud of the pot against her skull. She died instantly.

Then, the dazed man turned, trying to come after me. However, a loud explosion resounded from the other room, knocking him to his knees before Severo Ignacio's feet. His stiff arms extended forward, placing a perfect shot in the middle of his cranial implant.

"See you around," said Ignacio.

"See you soon," I replied.

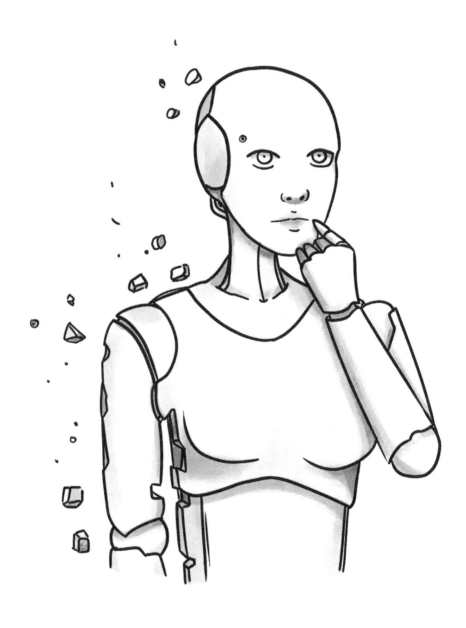

Crow 8

Luke Comes from the Future

I forgot to tell you that my name is Luke Patterson. I'm a professor of the History of Ancient Earth department at the virtual College of the Great Global Community. Before we get started, I apologize for the abrupt way in which I interrupted your reading. First of all, I need to explain to you that I come from the year 2235, from the Mount Phillips Megaplatform, a transoceanic construction that allows those of us who have been implanted to live on the ancient planet Earth, your planet Earth, with the few natural resources that remain under the control of the new global order.

We 800,000 inhabitants of the planet are divided into twelve other megaplatforms, and we share our daily lives with the humanoids created by Amber Technologies to simplify our most complicated tasks without needing to exhaust so many organic resources.

The androids were created by the last North American corporation, NEX (North American Emporium X) to defend the planet from alien occupation by the Kiplarians. In truth, we cannot call it an invasion, since the Kiplarians were in Antarctica long before the dinosaurs; however, with the melting of the glaciers caused by global warming, sea levels rose so dramatically that in a period of forty years, all vestiges of terra firma on the planet disappeared, leaving the people of Kiplar-B visible to all. Nevertheless, after the negotiations and the signing of the International Reunification Agreements, the Kiplarians, aligned with the great financial elites of the world, gave rise to Amber Technologies, the power nexus of the new, advanced societies. Then, they began to

71

build megaplatforms with the use of extraterrestrial technology, and we managed to survive the apocalypse.

The implantees—as we humans fitted with the cranial chip are now called—have learned to breach the time barrier, and today, I have come via the most economical way possible of doing this, thanks to the pen of a writer galloping over his history. I shouldn't explain this because it is not our main objective here, but if I had done it in person, it would have turned out to be costlier, and besides, you would have experienced a great shock. Just as in your times, we professors are poorly paid, and so I try to apply the reduction in neurocoins to complete my thesis. No great surprise to you, I imagine.

On the other hand, it is not my intention to cause panic with a holographic image or one that is completely materialized in the body of a human being of your era. That is something only the scientists at Amber Technologies can do. They can permit themselves the luxury of coming and going as often as they like, and when they do, generally, they occupy the body of some good-for-nothing, one of those who go around deceiving people with cheap pamphlets. Therefore, my dear reader, there is no charge for my warnings about the bluster of your times. You won't think it strange that in this advanced society, where a piece of news takes just a few seconds to travel through the cranial chips of the entire global population, where we can make purchases with an app that is activated with a thought command, and where the new global order knows exactly when your next visit to the bathroom will take place, that human suffering remains basically the same, but with more technology. Imagine, then, a Society of Idiocy 2.0.

There is no doubt, then, that serious scientists like me exist, as do lowlifes who sell themselves to push certain research studies that favor large corporations. More than a hobby, time travel for me means the development of a doctoral dissertation titled "The Origins of the Great Global Community." Because there are some who maintain that Kiplarians are responsible for our human misfortunes. Others, even more daring, believe that humanity's destiny has been written since the beginning of time. In my case, I suspect that man has always sought to place the blame for his own self-destruction on anything at all. My thesis, contrary to what you may think, is not a theoretical or philosophical dissertation, like those written in your era, but rather behavioral evidence that allows us to prove the hypothesis and that, besides, can be sent telepathically in a matter of seconds. What a task I've got, right?

And yet, to validate my study, and given that I have already explained my visit to you in the greatest detail possible, all I ask is that you respond mentally to four simple questions. Can you help me?

Starting transmission:

Name of thesis author: Luke Patterson

I.D.#: CG-872763A

Department: History of Ancient Earth

Year Access Requested: 2022.

Status: Basic authorization.

Sending question #1…

In what way are most children being raised in the year 2022?

Option 1: With the guidance and affection of their parents.

Option 2: With the stimulus of reading, the arts, and culture.

Option 3: With a "mobile phone" in their hand most of the day.

Registering your reply…Question completed.

Sending question #2…

What do people do when they finish drinking from a plastic bottle?

Option 1: Place it in a recycle bin.

Option 2: Keep it and wait for a chance to dispose of it appropriately.

Option 3: Throw it into the street or into a general trash can.

Registering your reply…Question completed.

Sending question #3…

How do most people spend more than half their time?

Option 1: Enjoying quality time with their family.

Option 2: Developing their intellectual capacity.

Option 3: Glued to a mobile phone like technology zombies.

Registering your reply…Question completed.

Sending last question.

Imagine this situation: A person from the year 2022 is drinking a glass of water and doesn't want to finish the contents. This person then proceeds to:

Option 1: Save the water for later.

Option 2: Use the rest to water the trees.

Option 3: Spill the water down the first drain he finds.

Registering your last reply…Question completed.

Thank you very much for your participation and for contributing to my thesis. To conclude, I will say goodbye now, because I suspect that my thesis will require more work. But first, I would like to share with you the replies that other people from your era have sent me. Processing access to data bank and previous statistics…

Question #1: In what way are the majority of children in the year 2021 being raised?

Option 1: With the guidance and affection of their parents. 98%.

Option 2: With the stimulus of reading, the arts, and culture. 1.5%.

Option 3: With a "mobile phone" in their hand most of the day. 0.5%.

Question #2: What do people do when they finish drinking from a plastic bottle?

Option 1: Place it in a recycle bin. 97.5%.

Option 2: Keep it and wait for a chance to dispose of it appropriately. 1.5%.

Option 3: Throw it into the street or into a general trash can. 1%.

Question #3: How do most people spend more than half their time?

Option 1: Enjoying quality time with their family. 49.5%.

Option 2: Developing their intellectual capacity. 49.5%.

Option 3: Glued to a mobile phone like technology zombies. 1%.

Question #4: Imagine this situation: A person from the year 2021 is drinking a glass of water and doesn't want to finish the contents. This person then proceeds to:

Option 1: Save the water for later. 50%.

Option 2: Use the rest to water the trees. 45%.

Option 3: Spill the water down the first drain he finds. 5%.

Thank you for reading me. Now, I must return. I have already expended a great amount of energy on this connection. When we receive the results of this study, I think I will have to invest more resources in continuing to look for elements that will help me prove my hypothesis. According to the replies received, apparently, up to the year 2022, people have not been responsible for the destruction of the planet. We will therefore continue to blame the Kiplarians, the politicians, or anything that makes our lives more comfortable.

Crow 9

Barbarito Bond

Your life won't be the same after reading these lines because you will have, in your hands, the story of a universally unsung hero.

You don't believe me? You've undoubtedly never heard of anyone who was capable of killing his boss' dog without the boss finding out. A gray pitbull with diabolical eyes. And it didn't belong to any old boss, either. In truth, life is too short to spend it hanging around with a bum. We're referring to the director of the FBI.

And if you're still reluctant to appreciate the magnitude of what I represent, just imagine a glass jar—the kind they sell at the market, minus the tomato sauce—covered with dust and steel screws, as many as they could fit in before closing the lid. I must confess that this wasn't the way the dog died. It's the way those two good-for-nothings disappeared—the ones who thought they were going to make a fool of me. They exploded into pieces inside the elevator. Then, the elevator was closed to the public because who would want to get into one of those things, knowing that somebody's guts were hanging from everywhere?

At sixty-something, I don't live a real life like the kind everyone hopes to have. I don't go around babysitting grandkids, or watering tulips, or feeding the pigeons in the square. That's also for poor slobs. My age is the perfect mask to hide the danger I carry inside. That's my nature. Skilled, fast, lethal. I can take a Glock apart with a single hand without anybody noticing. To do that, you need the natural gift that only the illuminated have, and great military preparation, as well.

This instinct was the only one that would allow me to find out that, after the alarms went off, the whole building would start to smell like burnt barbecue. The commotion not only affected several floors, but several blocks, as well. The cameras on the fifteenth floor might have captured the glorious moment, but someone who's prepared and knows what he has to do can't commit that kind of error.

"A terrorist attack! A terrorist attack!" screamed the old lady in 23B, who ran from her apartment unsteadily, and with no brakes. Grab her!

She even forgot her sciatica, and—imagine!—it's twenty-three floors down! As if, after an explosion like that, everybody's going to have a chance to escape, running. Or like my neighbor, Arnoldo. He opened his door and asked if someone had just knocked.

"For fuck's sake, Arnoldo! Put that thing in your ears; didn't you hear the cannon shot? Get back inside, man, that was an explosion!"

In any case, if there's anything I know how to do, it's acting crazy; so, I headed back inside the apartment with Lucía, ignoring the shouts of astonishment behind the closed door of the senior apartment building on Collins Avenue.

In actuality, I hear better than you'd think. I walk better than you'd think. I live better than you'd think. That was why I sat down to watch Don Francisco with his characters, Chacal and La Cuatro, uncorking laughter among the fake assistants, until the guys from the rescue squad, tired of knocking at my door, knocked it down, only to find me in my bathrobe, stretched out on my brown leather recliner, cracked from the sun, and chewing gummy candies shaped like animals, which work best for my false teeth. I pretend to be asleep and unaware of anything special going on. I used to enjoy peanuts—the kind that come in a little red bag—but I can't eat them as easily as I once did because it's hard to unstick them from my teeth.

The officer who approached me took my pulse before waking me. I don't know why the hell they have that prejudice against old folks who sleep in a chair. Listen, dude, I'm asleep. I'm not going to die scratching my balls! They can be sure of that. That middle-aged officer asked me to come with him to evacuate the building, just when the Chacal blew his trumpet and the bathrobe got tangled up with my left nut, revealing my you-know-what. At sixty-something, it's not so easy to get up from a chair. Though it is easy to forget to put on underwear before slipping on a bathrobe. That good man pretended not to see anything, because really, what guy doesn't take the hint when he sees another guy's dick? What's he supposed to say? "Nice dick"? or "Don Barbarito, your johnson is showing"?

Besides, I imagine he was worried because some hit man whacked two lowlifes in the elevator of an old folks' home. And that, my friend, is something you don't see every day in Miami. On the other hand, in this country, every explosion, no matter how small, inevitably makes people think—like the old broad in 23B—of a terrorist attack. They don't even think that minutes before, I had just gotten out of that elevator, and I had all the answers they were looking for.

Slow as a tortoise. The agility that characterizes me can't be found in that walker with wheels I bought to distract abusers. And besides, I won't deny it, so that they would take care of me. My real agility is in what I think about. When some youngster of eighteen thinks about doing me harm, I have a plan at the ready to pull down his pants and give him two smart slaps. Then, I grab the walker again and that's that, my man! I accuse him of being a pervert.

The truth of the matter? I could've done it without the walker, but it's just that I got tired of making my lunch every day and of people thinking I can still go to the office and see Jackson's face, Monday to Friday, turning in reports that the idiot doesn't even read.

Too bad about the elevator; it got stained with shit. Those two morons thought they could escape unharmed from an encounter with Lucía, the building's cleaning lady. My Lucía. Enormous butt. Once in a while, I let go of the walker so she can see that I can still do it. In fact, every day at 1:00, I walk by the laundry room in the hall to say hi and give her another little pat on the ass.

"Ay, Don Barbarito, you're terrible!"

"Lucía, a little kindness at any age is appreciated."

"But...are you still active, man?"

"Just let me take my hands off the walker and you'll see how this old guy rocks..."

It all ended in laughter. She thought I was playing. But I wasn't. I thought she liked me. Logically, she didn't want to get involved in problems with a sexagenarian. You know, to protect her twelve-peso-an-hour job. Or maybe more? Or, "God forbid old man Barbarito goes and has a heart attack on me." One of those seizures that leaves no room for a next time.

I'll try anything. As far as I'm concerned, there was no problem. I had already discussed it with my cardiologist, Dr. Narváez Pinzón of the Forever Young Medical Center.

"You take half of one of these pills, half an hour before the party, and you'll turn into a monkey with his dick swinging. But no more than a half, Barbarito; don't go overboard."

"Listen, doc, that little pill isn't dangerous for my ticker, is it? I mean, you know I'm a healthy guy and I'm physically prepared for these things, but just in case..."

"No worries, Barbarito. Follow the instructions and light up those eight cylinders of yours."

Lucía had the hots, and I had the hose to put out that fire. But that day, two delivery men, kind of odd-looking and wearing Postal Service uniforms, were poking around the halls of the building. I had spotted them, grumbling, and looking for doors, like they didn't really want to be there, but they had no packages in their hands. Poor dudes. They burned to a crisp in the elevator. With more holes than a sieve and smelling like carbon and vinegar. But Lucía was spared, and that's the most important thing. Thirty years of service in the FBI told me that those two guys were involved in strange stuff—Vietnam, Korea, Angola, Afghanistan, Panama. I've never been to those countries, but hell! I was here offering intelligence assistance from the office, filing documents, creating reports, and classifying the bad guys. That counts too, right? Well, maybe not, go fuck yourself, Jackson.

I wanted a little action, to flash my creds, impress the ladies, get a VIP pass to the World Series. The Marlins against the Indians, and in extra innings. Rentería, the Colombian baseball player, hits a fastball to center field—and we were the champs! I didn't see it because of that damn Jackson and his shitty office. I had just one year left before retirement, and I never received a foreign commission or a tough interrogation. Or any of the federal shit that was worth looking at and where I could demonstrate all my military abilities: body-to-body combat, arms management, and all the things we were prepared for to protect our fatherland. Even with Günter as a buddy. What the fuck!

Oh, that Günter! As a buddy, he was just about as useful as a fan ripped from the ceiling. He was useless. They would send him out to make photocopies and he'd come back minus the originals. That's why they had him serving coffee in the warehouses on the first floor. Thinking about that bothers me even more because I really do have infantry training in the Navy, but Jackson had me doing the same work as Günter, only one floor up. He never gave me the promotion I deserved, even if I was first out of all the trainees of agent school.

And even so, my cat, Kiki, stuck with me through all the failures. Seeing papers tossed into the wastebasket beside my desk and watching over it until the office lights went out, around 11:00, smelling of tar and tired of frozen pizzas from the vending machine on the second floor. The most exciting thing I recall about those offices was when a raccoon climbed up to the ceiling and I had to chase it away with a broom. But the little bastard got away and shit on the brand-new silk shirt that my daughter had given me for my fifty-something birthday. I made a soup out of that fucker. Luckily, it was early morning. I was on guard duty that day, which is the same as saying it was my turn to watch the re-runs of the Don Francisco show, eating nachos with salsa, cheese, and jalapeños, while Jackson frolicked with his little lady, telling her about the war he was waging against me.

There was a moment when I felt that my role in the FBI was like El Chacal with Don Francisco. They never saw my face, and besides, he carried a trumpet in his hand all the time. That poor wretch, Jackson. If only he knew that I was the one who killed that flea-bitten guy with the face of one possessed. Yeah, well, that's kind of a long story because Jackson decided to invite the whole department to his house, to a New Year's Eve dinner back around 1999. I never made it to that party because that fucking pitbull he kept in the yard wouldn't let me in. It barked and barked and barked. Its eyes were as red as two volcanos. Those animals, when they bite, they don't let go, and I wasn't about to fuck up the Sherlock outfit I had bought myself for five hundred dollars with the annual bonus they gave us at the office. Ah…I remember that I spent it with pleasure, so I would shine as the most successful FBI agent that night. Real authority. So that everyone would see how a real lone wolf should look, the most dangerous man ever to step on the agency's grounds. A suit consisting of a yellow jacket, with an impeccable white cashmere beret, perfectly harmonizing with a pair of equally white leather shoes, highly shined and without socks. I looked down at the floor, just so I could comb my hair. When I walked, I smelled the background scents:

Ay candela, candela, candela me quemo ahí!

"And the pitbull, chico, it wouldn't let me through! I shouted at the door of the house, as if it could hear me."

That's why you shouldn't complicate things, man. No point in going round and round with poor slobs. A Walmart steak with plenty of acetaminophen dressing, and fuck everything. Fuck Jackson and his pitbull. Next to the dead dog, I left him a grubby Yankees cap that I bought for two dollars from a drunken Cuban who happened to be passing in front of the house. He believed the story that I was Compay Segundo and that I was coming from a tour in Miami. What a load he had on, caballero!

Then, I hopped into my '87 Chevy and headed for a secret brothel at Calle Ocho. With my classy outfit and the five hundred bucks I still had in my pocket, I was going to live the good life. Later, that nice little jacket got smeared with lipstick, but what can you do? I forgave the bar girl, but what about Jackson's pitbull?

I remember they called me "007" at the brothel that night. The girls were laughing. All of them wanted to make it with me. I became the sheikh of Calle Ocho. The emir of Pinar del Río. Man! I went around all puffed up by what I imagined was my resemblance to James Bond. But Sean Connery's Bond, not those assholes they have nowadays. You know, tall, good-looking, with that air of a mercenary with deep pockets. A little darker, sure, but since I was an FBI agent, the girls flooded the room, all worked up with emotion. They ordered bottles of rum with their hands raised, and after a little while, I had three of them sitting on my lap. Then, I adjusted my beret at an angle and looked all around with a serious expression, as if I were watching out for the danger that can lie in wait anywhere, and I said to them, "Put both your hands on the wheel; I'm a very nervous passenger."

All of them sighed. That bar could drive a man crazy. Some of the guys who were there that night paid and left. I must admit, though, that after an argument with one of the girls, she got annoyed and told me that they called me "007" because I only lasted seven seconds before I came. Man, what a bitch that bar girl was!

Ay! What do I care about envy, caballero? Fact is, people don't appreciate real style, but of course, that's what I get for hanging out at those places on Calle Ocho. Afterwards, when I was left without a buck to my name, I left that brothel like a shot, or maybe they threw me out, without the beret, because I couldn't find it. That was the next day, around 12:00. Then, I slept off my hangover in the parking lot, inside the Chevy. After waking up around 5:00 in the afternoon and eating some shit at the McDonald's on the corner, I went home to wash off the brothel smell and to keep watching Don Francisco sprawled out in the recliner that Kiki occupied when I wasn't there. I checked a few messages from my colleagues on my answering machine, in which they asked me why I hadn't gone to Jackson's party. And it's just as well I didn't go because it all got fucked up when they had to go out and apprehend a drunken beggar who had killed the dog. They call it Federal Intelligence.

"Those green eyes…As peaceful as a lake…" I love that song. And when Ibrahim sings it, well, turn everything off, caballero! Because I'm going to dedicate it to Jackson's dog. And to the other animal, also!

Do you know what it's like to retire at sixty-something and all they give you is one of those diplomas that the secretaries print out in offices? Ah, fuck that! And some crappy ring that didn't even fit me because the son-of-a-bitch got my finger size wrong.

"We are all gathered here to recognize the work of a great agent who is retiring today, Barbarito Fuentes, who, over these thirty years of service has been an example for all of us. More than a colleague who has given everything in the service of his nation, he has been a great friend." Bullshit, bullshit, and more bullshit. I closed my eyes to pretend I felt like crying, when what I was thinking was how could I run like a flash to the brothel to celebrate the fact that I'd never again have to see the face of that idiot who ruined the brilliant career of the best FBI agent this country has ever known? Let's see now, you piece of shit, if you can figure out my ring size with this finger shoved up your ass! That's why, caballero, I don't pick fights and I take my walker with me everywhere. So that no one will suspect the real deadly weapon that lurks behind my cotton guayaberas, or the nine millimeters I carry pressed up against my disposable adult diaper and the Swiss army knife I wear tied around my ankle.

The day of the explosion at the building, the police officer, like a decent man, pretended not to see my weapon. But what he didn't even suspect is that if Lucía hadn't thrown in that grenade bottle and pulled me out by the walker before the elevator doors closed, I would have been responsible for giving two Russian agents, disguised as delivery men, their just rewards. Two hours earlier, they had overtaken me at the entrance to my apartment. Doubtless, they wanted to torture me or take me to some foreign country so that I would spill everything about the national secrets I learned in my thirty years of service with the FBI.

Or is it possible they were only after the white shoes?

Crow 10

Desideratum

Very few hours now separate me from my departure, and even so, I just wait and wait, my eyes fixed on the radio alarm clock. No one would understand if I told them that I've always known that today would mark my time to leave. I concealed it for years, or perhaps it didn't matter too much to them, since nobody ever knocks at the door.

Perspiration. That exciting gossip who begins her task by dampening the pillow and forcing me to get up, resting both feet on the naked earth, absent the summer scent of their neighbors. And so I wait, of course, beneath the roof of dried leaves from the inner forest for what is coming, far from my wattle-and-daub dwelling, ignited by the noonday heat. No wonder my mother always told me that no one should die in the heat of the sun, because that made the souls overheat. And an overheated soul will then refuse to go.

Despite my hurried pace, I knew I would die with altruistic elegance, far from the showy ceremonies of the capital, of the caravans with their endless splendor, and of the professional mourners. An empty declaration: Look, an asshole just died!

That's not how an important person meets his death.

"Get this straight, Carlitos. Right now, you might not understand much, but your grandfather's blood will remind you of it forever."

Because it's easy to sell a needy body's laughter, but it's also easy to finish off its tears. That's not the way to see off famous men, peeing on their dignity at an altar of obligatory offerings. And so, those who endure over time, those who remain in the memories of the ones who remain behind, don't need to make a lot of noise to accompany their departure. They go and that's it.

Simón Bolívar, the great liberator of nations.

Edgar Allan Poe, the great liberator of letters.

And Vidal Romero, the great liberator of exploited women.

Alone, but not forgotten.

That's how I want it to be written. But with capital letters and without shame. A silent departure is the best revenge for cold hearts. I'd bet on it. In fact, I bet on everything. We, who are a different size, risk our lives without discord, crowded by the indifference of other people's doubts. They call us crazy. Tossed out of windows by those vehement ballasts of ignorance, who walk through life as though it would last them forever. They run away from themselves, disguised in false intelligence. Without any capacity or merit for facing the end, with a bottle of Appleton Estate resting on their chest and two well-secured gonads, despite their patched underwear. As my compadre Alfonso would say, may God preserve him ready to receive me, "Nobody struggles with his craw full of someone else's rum."

Death is pure philosophy. No fuss or bother. Who but the living fear that deep sleep? Could I have died sometime? Hey, man, what a great question!

Dead, those who don't think about their legacy to eternity. Dead, those who forget easily, without footsteps in their pursuit. *"Non metuit mortem qui scit contemnere vitam"* side by side with Cato's Latin on lost farms. An embrace at the end so that he may feel the warmth of the decisive men beside him.

"911. Please state your name, age, and location."

"Hello, Miss. I'm Vidal Romero, age sixty-two, and I'm on Route 25 in Lancaster, the last house at the edge of the embankment. In front of the house, there's a white sign with a monstrosity that identifies it: 'For you, Cecilia,' or 'For your sake, Cecilia.' Something like that."

"How can we help you, Mr. Romero?"

"How can you help me? Well, I'm going to die in twenty minutes, and I'm with Carlitos, my seven-year-old grandson," he says in a quiet voice.

"What do you mean by 'die'? Could you give me more details?"

"More details about my death?"

"Are you alone? Besides the boy, is someone else with you?"

"It's just the boy, death, and me."

"In case you're being threatened, tell me what time it is."

"It's 8:48 PM."

"Don't move, Sir, and don't hang up the phone."

Without hanging up, but silencing my phone, I check, once again, the quarter of whiskey left in the bottle. At the same time, I try to remember the last dumb thing I said about death, and I also verify on my phone—just in case—that thirty-nine was really the sixth number. That same number which, together with the five previous ones, allowed me to prove that I'm the only winner of the "Super Millionaire" lottery. Yes, on the screen of the tiny phone that I've seen fall so many times since 2012, when I bought it after Carlitos' birth.

To die when there are reasons to stick around—how poetic! A loud thud and here's where I should fall. I hope the hammock doesn't get stained. It's not responsible for my destiny. To die alone is seductive; well, only if you know something about seduction.

Let me see, man…Five, nine, seventeen, twenty-eight, thirty-five and…yes…thirty-nine, though that three looks like an eight on the edge of that glass, broken by a blow.

I don't trust myself because of my promiscuity with booze, but we famous folk get drunk, too; so, I ask Carlitos to bring me my glasses, which are right there, beside the clothesline. I imagined he would arrive home on tiptoe, but the little cord didn't even move. It won't be the end after I go, and I'll return to remove that little cord from the banister. If I loosen it now, the clothesline will fall, with all the clothes, right on top of the boy. C'mere, little man, it's best if you don't bring them to me. You see what it says here? I can't hear you. What does it say? Yes, that's exactly it: thirty-nine. Son! Because you're like a son to me, Benedetti's scar of love.

"Mr. Romero, are you still on the phone?"

It's $355,000,000 before taxes. A lot of money, even for someone who won't be able to spend it tomorrow. I'll stop drinking the Appleton that Navarrete had in the office, until it's time for me to go. A lovely scent of fine Jamaican wood.

Why didn't anybody ever mention anything about the relevance that people who die drunk acquire? It's like a celebration in advance, which, if it could talk, would crucify all the lovers of faggoty mourning beforehand.

"Vidal is dead! Vidal is dead!"

Take a seat on the pedicle of my statue. I'll be watching you from on high, looking down with my hand stuck between the two buttons on my stone shirt. There, you'll have time to lie down calmly with your little black handkerchiefs.

For Carlitos, it's a pity that it's my turn today. That's life. I don't decide these things. If I did, his mother wouldn't have died during childbirth. But having accidentally bought that lottery ticket was a good deed on the boy's part. Nice way to bid farewell to the only being who recognizes him as his real and only grandson. That's what kids are like today: they fool around with mobile phones and do everything better than the old folks—from calling people you don't want to talk to, to accidentally buying a lottery ticket.

"Mr. Romero!"

"I'm sorry, they're asking me to hang up."

"Who's asking you to do that? How many people are there? Mr. Romero!"

Come here, my boy. I need to give you a hug. You've brought me great joy (355,000,000!) Now, I realize that Cecilia didn't love me. Or you, either. I think she was never able to recover from your mother's tragic death. But I did take care of you, while she, in the most casual way, arranged the divorce papers with Dr. Navarrete and the papers for the house in Palo Alto. She colluded with the lawyer and even went to live with him. In vain, because like a good lawyer, he has no word, and in a month's time, he left her, with her age and her singlehood, and I think he even took her house away. She denies it. She wants me to believe that she's still with him. She doesn't answer my calls. She doesn't know that I'm just calling to say goodbye. We don't interest her, Carlitos.

"Whatever you may need from me, discuss it with Navarrete! He's the one who represents me now," she screamed, all full of herself.

She opened that enormous maw of hers, just to breathe out the last name of that hustler, though there's no denying she has good taste in rum. You can tell she makes good money by scamming dotty old ladies. And she thought she had robbed me of something great, but she doesn't know that I stole other things from her house, the day we signed the divorce papers, when I went to use the bathroom. Man doesn't live by peace alone. And neither do the deaths of famous people depend on pointless sacrifices. Ah, Robert Louis Stevenson, "Fifteen men on a dead man's chest/ Yo-ho-ho and a bottle of rum."

Cecilia couldn't stand so much pain, and I can even understand her, but...to tell me that nothing about you interested her? This is the strange world I have to say farewell to, because despite the barbarity of her indifference and her betrayal with the shyster lawyer, what tears my soul most is to think that I knew her, but now, I admit I do not. The truth shines through the wretchedness; it pushes it aside to glow in the most hidden corners. There mustn't be any soul in a heart that's capable of rejecting a seven-year-old child, with her own blood running through his veins. No matter how much mischief he may have committed.

"Do you remember, Carlitos? You grabbed her phone on many occasions and called the cemetery to ask for your mom. One time, you transferred two thousand dollars to an account at a casino, and then you called 911 to report that someone was beating you."

And this hammock that doesn't tie properly. Don't look at me that way, boy. What difference does it make? I've never really liked drinking until very late, but I suppose I shouldn't worry about having a headache tomorrow. Even that dies along with death. This ranch will belong to you; when you grow up, you may need it to drown those dark moments. Or to lock away a woman. Do you like women? They taste like chocolate. When you're a little older, you'll understand me. Also: soliloquy. They work very well here. Burning coal, palm fronds, and murky heat to keep the hammock wet. Beer? Never drink it because it'll give you a big belly.

"Hello? Is this Dr. Navarrete? Vidal Romero speaking… Look, I'll be brief, Doc. As you can see, I've just sent you a screenshot that shows today's lottery ticket. It's on my phone, and yes, I won. It's just one ticket. But what you're going to hear after this call will be a shot to my head. If you get here before the police, you can pick up my phone along with the winning ticket. It's all yours! What? Have I gone crazy No, no, no…I think you don't understand me; excuse the drama of this message. I love Cecilia, and I'd do anything to see her happy. So, if her happiness is with you, and as I know she doesn't answer my calls, well, accept these $355,000,000. And, well, on with the show! I've decided to die today anyway."

As soon as the police arrived at the hut, they found Dr. Lucio Navarrete in slippers, removing an empty bottle of Appleton Estate from the corpse, and hiding the weapon that days before had been stolen from his house. There was no one else in the room.

Crow 11

Conversation of Tears

It seems like a perfect day to converse with tears, but before the abundance of her majestic, cottony, white curls, I have decided to remain scattered, fearless, unflappable, awaiting the breath that inspires everything I've felt until now. Her presence calls me—seduces me to leave off everything I am because of her, to return to her as if propelled toward the sky, and all because of the passion of her gaze.

I must confess that despite my years and hers, she has always made me float in this way. It's her merciless flame that makes me burn with desire inside. It disperses it into a thousand pieces; she wraps them in her velvety arms, where I am happy, not only because now I am with her, nor because I have found a reason to start again, but because I belong to her once more. My urges calm down when I compress myself within her cold breasts, damp from so many caresses with the ecstasy of each climax.

Then, the tears, copious from so much emotion, surrender to their encounter and don't want to converse anymore. Clinging to her life is my only option for continuing to breathe heavenward with all my being, in a melody that comes from deep love, from stories that have been so worn out in the retelling that they will never end.

But the truth is that she is tired of so much loving and wants no more of it. And I don't want her pity.

I can't bear to see her weep from ennui in my presence, because each expelled tear carries my pain of losing her in uncontrolled downpours of deep love. She can reject me, push me away a thousand times, and I will keep loving myself alone, knowing I will possess her, although others may have made her forget me.

My downfall will not know how to say goodbye.

The pain will tighten me from all sides and from nowhere at the same time.

What I carry within me belongs more to her than to me, and that has to continue to be so. The blow will make me live in a different form, in another flower to cry with, and even with other tears lost in seas of loneliness. I will fall, only to scatter into heartbroken spurts, feeding the hopes of those who hope to absorb me in the depths of their infinite thirst.

It seems like a perfect day to converse with tears about everything she has meant to me. In the end, there will always be room in my heart to converse but never to forget her. It will not be easy to turn into passing squalls or into the river that follows its channel, as if nothing had happened. Emptiness, too, overflows in the sentence of those shed tears as well as in those that are hidden, those that suffer, and those that end up like us, separated by different worlds and condemned by the simplicity of their existence.

I was that white cloud, and even though now, I flow easily over the ground of eternity, I will return with more tears to find her.

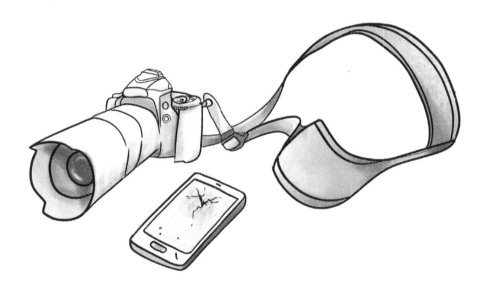

Crow 12

Where is Jack Rickshaw?

It seems that it wasn't the first time he was visited by the aliens. And yet, before the last brilliant spark the sky offered him on that cold November night in New York, Jack Rickshaw fell to his knees and was never seen again.

It happened on the main balcony of the headquarters of *The Manhattan Post*, at 10:13 PM, to be exact. Nothing else can be seen in the video, since at the moment his knees simultaneously hit the ground, his phone fell from the fifteenth floor, spinning like a wound-up top. There were no screams. Just the incandescent spark of what looked like a humanoid silhouette, fuzzily outlined behind his panicked eyes. That was all the mobile phone could offer us as it spun.

"Where is Jack Rickshaw?" was the front-page headline on that 24th of November 2021. Many accused the newspaper of yellow journalism. Others went even farther. The editors of *The New Yorker* rushed to produce an afternoon edition, suggesting that Rickshaw was just on a forced vacation, since Antoine Zimmerman, the editor-in-chief, had fired the southerner hours earlier because of his incapacity to cover events that deserved more attention. But they had to prove that the video was a fake—a very difficult thing to do because all the experts agreed with what their eyes had seen.

"Rickshaw! My office! What the hell is going on with you? Why did Goodman get the scoop on Ben Affleck and JLo? Do they think we were the ones behind that photo?"

"They paid, Antoine."

"And why the hell didn't we pay? Jack, I'm really tired of your stupid blunders. I can't explain these things! *The New Yorker* has Goodman on every damn corner in Manhattan, and your butt doesn't fit in the chair from all those donuts you stuff in your mouth. Roberts, my office!"

"Oh, yeah! Here comes Clark Kent…"

"If you had Roberts' guts, the whole damn department would be lined with Pulitzers. Joe, how's the piece on President Porter's divorce coming along?"

"The former First Lady will give us the interview, and Rickshaw won't be President."

"Idiot…"

"Is one of López's people following this?"

"Yeah. Barry has tried to get the interview through the Secretary of State, but the Former First Lady wants us to be the ones to discuss the divorce."

"Excellent. Have you covered Entertainment?"

"C'mon, Antoine, you can't leave me out of this. I've got the interview with Arctic Pinky locked up…Besides, I've practically got proof of the Secretary of Defense's affair in my hands."

"Shut up, Rickshaw! It's my ass that's on the line!"

"All right…I haven't done it, but I don't think there's anything complicated about a singer who only shows her panties live," Roberts said.

"Go to the Madison. Bring me the damn interview with Pinky. I need to calm the boss down and try to cover up the Goodman-López scoop a little. We're gonna bring 'em back everything…Jenkins! Hand me an aspirin, please. This damn day feels like it'll never end. And you, Rickshaw! I want you to get outta my office right now and go cover the grand opening of the New Jersey Zoo. Try to bring me an interview with the elephant, or the scoop on that monkey who writes with both hands. I don't know what the hell you're gonna invent, Jack, but you've got just twenty-four hours before I kick your disgusting ass out into the street."

"Are you serious, Antoine? To the zoo?"

"A scoop, Rickshaw! Just one…one fucking time…Ah! I almost forgot…I don't want any more of that extraterrestrial bullshit on my desk, unless you bring me photos of a little green man hugging Obama. And close the door when you leave!"

Minutes after that uncomfortable conversation, Rickshaw's cup of coffee was growing cold, forgotten on his desk. The mouse danced above the screen, looking for filed documents, opportunities with impending flashes in the shadow of his anxiety. The phone was tempting, but it also made him hesitate.

"Cristina, how're you doing?"

"Hi, Jack. Do you have a minute to talk?"

"Yeah, sure. Is the secretary about to speak?"

"Things have changed a little. I'll tell you later. In the light of such overwhelming proof, the president has decided he'll be the one to take charge of the matter personally. He's been advised not to beat around the bush and to remove Secretary Morgan before the scandal falls on his own head. This will give him some wiggle room for the next congressional elections. "

"Fantastic! When will he give me the interview?"

"Jack…the president wants Goodman…"

"No, Cristina, that's impossible. You must be joking…"

"I'm sorry, Jack. The decision's been made. The president is a little uncomfortable with *The Manhattan Post's* insistence on wanting to discuss his divorce with the former First Lady."

When he hung up the phone, Jack admitted that this would be the end of his fifteen-year career as a journalist.

At the Chief's office, Roberts and Zimmerman were exchanging banter and laughing at Jenkins' outrageous hairstyle, as if they were inseparable buddies; at least, that's what they looked like before the brown Venetian blinds were lowered. The rest of the office smelled of old paper. Plus, a little whiff of cigar, but that was the responsibility of the water ashtray belonging to Jenkins, an elderly secretary with a large birthmark above her mouth, and a heavy gait.

Jack needed time to breathe, to reorganize his thoughts a little. It was a given that he wouldn't be going to the zoo. It made no sense to comply with Zimmerman's punishment if the next day, at the same time, he would be fired—maybe sooner, if Goodman's interview was pushed up. He even thought about resigning, but he wouldn't give Roberts the pleasure of seeing him leave with his head hanging. Even worse, when he knew that *The New Yorker* had been bought months ago by an important Wall Street financial group, which allowed its financial department to pay off sources and even—a fact that no one would dare announce in public—to invent news that would guarantee the happiness of their supporters. Zimmerman knew it, but he'd never confirm it at the office.

"Too much coffee is bad for your nerves," Alice Hawkins said to Jack at the small office café. The beautiful reporter who covered sports stepped up to the hot water dispenser to prepare her customary chamomile tea.

"Chamomile makes me sleepy."

"At least it keeps you healthy. Zimmerman's intense today, isn't he?"

"He's an idiot."

"What's going on with your wife's kidnapping?

Jack sighed uncomfortably at a question he considered provocative.

"Really, Alice? You're on Roberts' side, too?"

"Not at all. I believe in your version of things. It's just that it'll have to be constructed around something tangible on the subject, you know? Zimmerman thinks that if he publishes something like that, the stockbrokers won't look on him favorably. Too bad you don't have anything solid."

"Thanks a lot. And what about you? How's it going with that Boston center fielder's transfer to the Yankees?"

"Nothing new. Jones' agent has called a halt to negotiations because of the cost of the rescission clause. He wants a bigger piece of the pie, and the kid doesn't know it. Are you going to the zoo?"

"I don't think so. That article won't be published anyway. I'm going to Chad's bar and having a couple of drinks to clear my head. Will you come?"

"Is this a date?"

"At Chad's bar? I don't think so. It wouldn't look very good on my part."

"And I wouldn't go out with a potentially unemployed guy."

Both of them laughed, but they agreed to meet at the bar to have a drink and escape from the office for a while. When he returned to his desk, Jack found a bunch of bananas with a handwritten note that said, "For the monkeys at the zoo." Everyone in the office laughed, including Alice, though she tried to brush it off a little with that typical gesture of her left hand covering her mouth. After picking up his overcoat from the old, wooden coat rack, Jack took the bananas and silently tossed them, annoyed, into the trash can, so as to leave the newsroom in a jolly state and head over to the bar.

Once in the elevator of the Groesbeck Tower, headquarters of *The Manhattan Post*, Jack picked up his cellphone to check his list of contacts. Abraham, Allison, Amber Pharmacy, Astudillo. Nothing interesting. Two more people accompanied him on his descent to the lobby of the tower. To his right, and in front of the controls, sat his friend Javier, the elevator operator. Slightly to the left and in front of him, he could see a middle-aged man, slender and with a long face. Black jacket, black eyeglasses, black gloves, black shoes. Even a parasol—also black. In his hand, he carried an old-fashioned briefcase, looking like it had been through many battles and connected strangely with a chain to a security bracelet on his right wrist. He had never seen him in the building before. That circumspect man turned to greet him with a simple grimace, a greeting from between clenched teeth. He looked Irish. It was evident that his left foot was bigger than the right.

When they reached the abandoned lobby, there were only six people. Three of them looked a little lost, trying to find the Costa Rican Embassy.

"It's on the fourth floor," he replied with unusual courtesy.

Jack never imagined that everything would change when he left that building.

THE BALCONY

It was around 4:00 in the afternoon, and everything was gray on an unusually cold New York afternoon. Unlike the lobby of the tower, the avenue revealed an intense busyness in both directions, while a police officer tried to control the random troupe of passersby, vehicles, and cyclists. A paragon of patience, that lawman. Trying to avoid an East Indian cabby attempting to start his car, I noticed how the strange man with the briefcase stood in front of the tower, waiting for someone, I imagined. I continued along my route for two more blocks, in search of Chad's famous bar. A small bar with lunches and beverages whose front window was covered by a red canvas canopy with an unmistakable logo: Chad's Bar. Under that canopy, faded by the inclement climate, was a place where Bohemians, writers, chess players, people engaged in festivities, and others, all gathered. In fact, at one of the tables set up for chess, the famous chess master, David Swanson, used to play back around 1976. That red-haired man with the manners of an introvert had allowed himself the luxury of defeating the then world champion, the Russian Andréi Ivanov. And I say 'tables set up for chess' because the chessboards were painted right on the table.

During my walk, I tried to recall some contact that might lead me to an important interview, or who knows what. However, the tumult of people crowding the sidewalk kept me from focusing my attention on my mind and even more importantly, on the sidewalk. Passing one block, I saw a group of three police cars and some firefighters standing in front of a famous department store. I tried to draw closer, but it turned out to be an elderly person who suffered from hypoglycemia. It wouldn't be news for me, so I went on walking.

"I'm on my way!" Alice texted me.

"Okay. See you there," I replied.

As I turned the corner, I could see the canopy of the bar, so I stuck the phone into my coat pocket and started to take off my gloves.

Once in the bar, I greeted Chad and took a booth for two in the back. It wasn't that I had any desire for Alice, but rather, I knew that our conversations needed to be as discreet as possible. First, however, I decided to go to the bathroom, also asking Chad to bring me a double whiskey on the rocks. I left my things on the table and walked down a narrow, dimly lit hallway to the end. A small table with an old-fashioned vase standing on it marked the space between the men's and women's restrooms. As I opened the heavy wooden door and huffed at the typical bathroom odor, I looked for one of those disposable urinals. I was the only person in the place, so I did my thing, at my leisure, with a sigh of relief and everything. But from outside the partition and in the space between the toilet and the floor, I could see a forgotten briefcase on the ground, which I immediately identified as belonging to the mysterious man in black from the elevator.

The improvised stall door was open, so it was just a matter of pushing it halfway to determine that there was no one inside, just the briefcase. The confusion of that fact disturbed me a little, and the only thing that occurred to me was to leave the restaurant to see whether I could find the man in black again and inform him that his briefcase was in the bathroom. But no. There were no traces of that man.

"How likely is it that the man got to the bar ahead of me?" I said to myself softly. "He came by car," I replied to myself almost immediately.

I decided to return to the bathroom to take the briefcase and hand it over to Chad because if that man had been carrying it while it was tied to his wrist, it must have been of the utmost importance to him. And yet, my intentions were in vain. The briefcase was no longer there.

"This is impossible! No one went into the bathroom while I was coming out."

My body started to shake because I could foresee that something wasn't right; I ran, even daring to explore the women's restroom, but there I found Alice, who was startled to see me.

"Hey, cowboy, you've got the wrong door."

"Yes, sorry, I was distracted. I'll see you outside."

"Listen, Jack. That man who's sitting at your table—did you invite him?"

"What man are you referring to?"

"A guy in black."

"You're saying there's a guy in black at the table?"

Alice nodded and I ran out after determining visually that there was no one else with her. When I got to the table, everything changed drastically.

"Chad!" I shouted, standing by my table. "Did you see that briefcase on my table?"

"Sure, I did. It was with you when you arrived. Then, you asked me for a double whiskey, and you went to the bathroom."

"What are you saying, man? You've never seen me with a briefcase."

"Yeah, it did seem strange to me. Good old Jack never carries a briefcase. I figured it must belong to the guy in black who arrived with you."

"Hey, guys, am I missing something?" asked Alice, emerging from the bathroom.

"It's Jack. He's been acting very strange lately. I think his work is affecting him a lot," said Chad, drying some glasses and arranging them on the tray at the bar.

"I think Chad is right, Jack. Do you want me to drive you home?"

"That briefcase …"

"What about the briefcase?" Alice asked.

"I think they're following me. We have to call the police."

"Wait…wait…the police? What for?"

After we sat down, I told her everything that had happened. We chatted non-stop for more than two hours. Surprised by the story, she made me understand that it might be a question of a hidden source attempting to divulge some extraordinary news. I knew she was right, but I wasn't sure I wanted to open the briefcase.

"Jack, this is your chance to have something good in your hands!"

"We don't even know what's in it, Alice. Don't you see it could be dangerous?"

"So, now you're afraid? Good reporters can't work with fear."

"Chad! Bring me two double whiskeys and a margarita."

"Don't bring him anything!" she said, gesturing to Chad with her hand. "Jack, you can't get drunk. You have to be sober to face whatever it is that's inside. Your career is at stake!"

"But it's just that…"

"Jack!" Alice shouted, striking the table. "Either you open it, or I'll take charge."

"Dammit, dammit, dammit! All right! I'll open it. But with two conditions. The first: you're with me in this."

"I'm already with you in this. And the second condition?"

"Chad! Two double whiskeys!"

"Goddammit, Jack!"

Time ticked along in our conversation. Chatting with the beautiful reporter had done me good, and I liked her. The clock on the bar now said 9:35 PM, and we had worked up our courage to open the briefcase. Alice picked it up and tried to pull off the strap, without success. She was nervous and could barely coordinate her hands; so, I pulled it away from her and, with a yank, I unfastened the strap that separated both of us from the mystery. Upon opening the flap, we saw that, beside a few meaningless papers, it was practically empty.

"But, what the hell?" I said indignantly.

"Wait—what's this?" asked Alice, pulling an elegant black handkerchief from the bottom of the briefcase.

I drank the second of the two whiskeys that Chad had brought me and quaffed it in a single gulp. Alice and I exchanged glances when we saw that, on one side of the fabric, there was a message clearly and hurriedly written in yellow ink that read: "Jack Rickshaw. 22:00. Balcony of *The Manhattan Post.*"

"I told you so, cowboy!" Alice shouted with anticipatory emotion. "Let's go! We've got to get over there."

"Do you think it's okay for you to come with me? It might be dangerous."

"Are you about to violate the condition you yourself added?"

She left me no choice. I called Chad over to total the bill and asked him to add it to my monthly tab. We left the bar with the briefcase in hand and hopped into a taxi. It was only two blocks away, but our haste and the extra whiskey prevented me from walking straight. I didn't want the news article to be something like: "Journalist Jack Rickshaw strolls around Manhattan in state of inebriation."

The East Indian taxi driver, whom I had evaded hours earlier as I left the tower, picked us up on the avenue and made ten dollars on that short trip. The night was dark. Very dark. Even clear. Very few clouds dared to perch in the sky that day. Alice and I entered the tower. We both had our official press I.D.'s, allowing us access to the office at any time of day.

When we arrived at the fifteenth floor, we left the elevator just as the electricity was cut off and the emergency lights in the hallway went on. Alice took my arm, as if seeking protection. I kissed her. It was an impulse, but I did it. She smiled. I pulled out my phone, turning on that light as best I could to find the electronic card reader at the entrance. I didn't know whether I should show my card from one side or the other. We were very nervous. When we finally got inside, there was no one in the newsroom. The journalists on duty were working from the other headquarters, because it was assumed they'd have better access to the eventual coverage.

The door to the balcony was open. Alice turned on the light on her phone to make her way to the bathroom, while I cautiously approached my desk. I laid the briefcase on the chair and removed my coat. I waited a few minutes for the girl to come out of the bathroom. However, she was taking too long.

"Alice, is everything okay in there?" I shouted from outside.

She didn't answer. I opened the door to the bathroom and saw that it was empty. Frightened, I ran away and saw her standing outside, on the balcony, with the briefcase in her hands.

"Alice, what's this all about? How did you get out of the bathroom without me seeing you?"

She didn't answer. She just turned around and pointed to the sky.

"Okay. This has gotten out of control. I'm going to get my phone and record everything that's happening. You'll understand that it's for my security."

Alice shook her head in protest.

Just after the phone started to record, she jumped from the balcony with the briefcase. I ran over to stop her, but I couldn't scream. Something I couldn't explain was suffocating me from deep inside. I reached the balcony and pointed to the sky. A strange, shiny object was moving in ways that completely defied gravity. I couldn't believe my eyes. My transmission immediately went viral, to the point of collapsing the network that was transmitting it. I fell to my knees before the immensity of the things that floated freely through the sky. The phone could no longer remain in my hands. Everything was extinguished, but not for long, I awoke on top of the counter of Chad's Bar. Everyone was dressed differently. Chad wasn't there. The calendar on the wall showed November 24, 2221.

"Hi, my name is Alice. Would the gentleman like something to drink?"

Crow 13

Terror at Lake St. Clair

The lock on the door is stuck.

Leaving might not be the best option, but I heard screams, and I'm sure they didn't come from my habitual nightmares. The floor is made of wood; it's frozen and very squeaky. The thick fog doesn't allow me to see out the window; so, I take my coat and throw it over my pumpkin pajamas. I try to loosen the lock with the handle of an old decorative cane that, seconds earlier, was resting on the flagstone wall that houses the chimney.

"I shouldn't have come," I say aloud.

Again, the gut-wrenching screams invade the cabin. A chill runs up and down my neck, and the cane falls over. Then, I head for the room where the lady is hidden and now lies on top of a red, felt blanket. She isn't breathing anymore; it's hard for me to breathe, too.

A gargoyle secured to her chest with both hands and an upside-down black cross at the foot of her bed invite me to flee in terror. Tumbling down the dark hallway, I shout, grief-stricken, and run toward one of the windows of the main room. It's sealed shut, and so are the others. The lock on the door confirms that I'm trapped, with only a cane and a rosary of golden beads.

"What's going on out there, Teresa?" I shout to my friend from inside the cabin. The dew on the windows begins to take on a red tinge.

"What the hell? This can't be happening to me!" I think, horrified.

The pale hands guide me through the darkness, and I remember that the candelabra doesn't work and that the gas lamp is outside with the adventurers. I sit down on the blue rug in front of the chimney to relax, when what I really want to do is hear Teresa tell me that everything is all right. That it's all part of a game they invented to frighten me.

What can you expect from a bunch of kids who spend Halloween night by the lake, keeping warm with glasses of cheap booze?

Beneath the chilling shadows, head lowered and hugging my bent knees, I rock back and forth. My sweaty fingers clutch the rosary beads. My breathing explodes, agitated, within a silence that can seem loud when the mind tries to flee from reality. The odor of the lake penetrates deep into my heart, making it beat violently. I don't want to look at the windows. I don't want to hear the screams. I don't want to rock back and forth anymore.

Behind me, the chimney walls start to creak. A thousand pieces of something slips from the ceiling. I get up, turn toward the chimney and run away toward the front door, my back turned. Both hands cover my surprised mouth, twisted in the most grotesque grimace of measureless panic. With my cabin door now very close, I trip over the cane with my left foot and recall that it's still on the floor. I bend down to grab it, and in a single movement, I stand, only to bang the lock with desperation that boils up from my stomach and floods my throat.

The cane is broken, but so is the lock.

I push the heavy wooden door away and try to flee, though not without first noticing the presence of an old leather Bible that is burning in front of the cabin with the remains of two glasses that flank it. I try to push them aside with the fragment of the cane, and somehow arrive at the shore of the lake.

"Teresa, where are you? Where did everybody go?" I cry, looking all around.

The cold flows from Lake St. Clair with breaths of infinite cruelty. Death announces that it's here, and I fall to my knees.

It's the dawn of the 31st of October 1988, when autumn has conspired with winter to confuse us all. Earlier, I had refused to stay outdoors with Teresa, Lucecita, Matt, their school friends, and the new girl, who had all decided to start a bonfire in front of Lake St. Clair. It was Teresa's idea, and after what I've just witnessed, I don't know if I'll be able to escape.

There was no other way for her to get her mother's permission to spend the night with Matt. I never liked that guy; neither did her mother. In all of Riverside College, Matt was the main topic of conversation—his new car, his parties in Rochester, and the basketball team, of which he was captain, of course. Lucecita seemed different. Unconcerned with popularity.

She was short and wore large bifocals that made her eyes seem to explode at the glance of any stranger. Despite my surprise and everyone else's, Lucecita had strange tattoos on her body, with a symbolism we never understood, since the girl seemed to be quite religious. Now, she was in the eye of the hurricane.

Teresa, on the contrary, took the lead in anything having to do with adventures. Slender, with green eyes, and a dark complexion that was irresistible to boys, she couldn't avoid being the center of attention in the corridors of Riverside, and she showed it off whenever she had the opportunity. It was my job and Lucecita's to divert that crazy girl whenever she had one of her "great ideas," and spending Halloween night at Lake St. Clair was one of those wild inspirations. Later on, things got a little bit complicated.

"Are you crazy? That boy just wants to show you off to his friends," I told Teresa.

"He's cute, girlfriend," she replied. "Or are you going to tell me you don't like to look at him in his tight basketball uniform?"

"Well, yeah. He's got his charm, but that doesn't mean he's not a jerk."

"Lucecita doesn't say anything, but her big eyes almost jumped over her lenses when she imagined Matt in his basketball uniform," she retorted, as all three of us burst out laughing at the same time.

To be honest, Lucecita seemed very embarrassed by the conversation.

We belonged to the church choir. We were the kind of girls you'd see in the classroom, the ones who hardly spoke, but who later forged their friendship as a consequence of coincidences in life. Lucecita attended church out of religious conviction and was the main singer in the choir. A real angel. Teresa's mom made her go to keep her away from bad influences. As for me, the two of them, working together, convinced me.

I had never thought about singing, though it was a huge surprise when my audition turned out to be a success. One stanza of "Oh, Merciful Praise" was enough to earn me a place among the sopranos. And yes. We celebrated my achievement in the least religious way possible.

Lucecita got drunk just remembering the incident, though Teresa's mom thought that the dinner at her house was the real celebration. In any case, the lamb in gravy was delicious, and everything played out in acts of friendliness and very amusing stories, though Teresa's dad was acting very strange. After staring insistently at Lucecita and me for the whole evening, he picked up his mysterious, round Bohemian glasses and retreated to his bedroom without saying another word. That same night, his wife gave each of us a beautiful rosary with shiny golden beads, asking us to carry them with us always to protect us from bad influences.

"They've been blessed by Father Jim," she said with unwavering Catholic pride. And we were delighted.

Dear Father Jim offered mass in the same church where we had our choir practice.

"God bless this choir of angels that heaven has sent us today!" said the kind septuagenarian.

With the rosary in her hand and after giving thanks for blessings received, Lucecita nodded, enraptured. I went before her. Teresa, on the other hand, asked her mom not to embarrass her in front of her friends anymore.

"God embarrasses you, Teresa?" asked her mother, looking her straight in the eye.

"No, Mom, but it's just that my friends and I..."

"Please, go back to your room. You need to give more thought to your relationship with God."

And at that moment, we realized that the celebration was over; so, we decided to go back to our homes, as well. But before that happened, Teresa's mom made an unexpected revelation that would change the path of our own relationships dramatically.

Matt's Corvette arrived at the fair, noisy, fast, and with the strident "Sweet Child o' Mine" blasting as if it were the last time he would hear it in his sad, idiotic life. Wearing a ridiculous, tight black leather outfit, he jumped out the car window, imitating some random rock star, though it was just Matt, the idiot. Teresa walked alongside him, and we all stood, mouths agape at the role of teen rebel she was playing. Seeing her, Lucecita grabbed me by the arm and adjusted her glasses. Looking at one another, we both decided to buy cotton candy to pretend we hadn't seen her and to assimilate the impact of that uncomfortable situation.

"Let's see what we've got here. Oh, yes! The ex-girlfriends who abandoned me to the punishment of the controlling mother."

"Teresa, where'd you get that outfit from? Why are you talking to us like that?" Lucecita asked.

"Look at Miss Prissy. The one who gets embarrassed by everything but squeezes her legs together when she sees my boyfriend."

"Don't talk to her that way!" I replied immediately.

"And Tina, the friend who slips into your house to flirt with your dad," Teresa shot back, pointing at me with an index finger that sported a very strange ring.

"That's it. We should go home. Let's go, Lucecita!" I said to my mortified friend. I turned to Teresa and said, "I don't know what the hell is wrong with you, but I'm sure that when you see Matt again, your lousy mood will go away."

That's what life is like among girlfriends. Sometimes, we fall victim to anger, but we always have one another's back. Matt helped the new girl into his Corvette, while Teresa snorted and walked away from the schoolgirls' pitying looks. Lucecita was the first to follow her, though not without first reminding Matt of what an idiot he was. I admit that I thought for a couple of seconds before following my bug-eyed friend. Teresa was furious.

Before the stream that flowed about one hundred meters from the fair, she removed one by one the items of clothing that, minutes before, had made her look ridiculous and which at that moment would disappear, swept along by the water.

"Get lost!" she shouted at Lucecita and me. "You're all a bunch of idiots!"

"We're here because of you, and you know it," I said as I grabbed her shoulder from behind.

"I should've known he would never fall in love with a crazy girl."

"Don't say that; you know it isn't true."

"My mom told you about my schizophrenia, didn't she? Leave me alone!"

"We won't do it."

"It's that new girl, the one with the cute little ribbon and the cute little voice. With that face like a cheap whore. She crawled her way into Matt's eyes."

"Matt is a jerk, and sooner or later, he would've fallen for her or anyone else," I remarked to Teresa.

"Tina, allow me," said Lucecita, pushing me aside with her arm in a way that surprised me.

"You're really stupid, Teresa. You let that goody-goody with the red ribbon steal Matt away from you!"

"Lucecita!" I shouted, surprised.

"She's right. I never slept with Matt because Teresa was his girlfriend," Lucecita went on, beside herself, as if something had taken possession of her. "My crotch gets wet whenever I see him, and you lost him!"

"Okay, this is getting out of control," I said to both of them.

Teresa turned around to look at Lucecita. They hugged and cried like two little girls who had lost their father. I still didn't understand, but at least everything was out in the open. I saw it in their gestures, and that made me feel calmer. I had been afraid that Teresa would do something stupid, and I know that Lucecita thought so, too.

Friendship is strange, and it can take on many forms when it comes to a girlfriend's pain. When you're a friend from the head, reason can make you keep your distance in difficult times. But when you're a friend from the heart, difficult moments strengthen you until your hearts blend into one.

Several days passed before Teresa could leave her room.

Her mother, very worried, spoke to Tina and Lucecita, asking them to visit her regularly. She insisted on the reality of her daughter's schizophrenic episodes. Tina, convinced that Teresa was sick, tried to care for her and not leave her alone. Lucecita, however, never believed in her illness, but remained with her until the end.

Things became complicated when Teresa's father fell into misfortune, the product of a legal accusation of trafficking of children's organs. Tina and Lucecita knew about it, but no one mentioned that subject at Teresa's house.

Matt had grown close to Teresa again, and she had rejected him on several occasions. Teresa's mother never found out about the episode at the fair, but still hated it when that boy came over to see her.

"Tina, is there something going on with that boy and Teresa?"

"No, Ma'am. He's an idiot and Teresa knows it."

"How long have they been going out?"

"I don't know. A couple of months."

Very nervously, she retreated to the kitchen, and Lucecita and Tina waited in the living room for Teresa to come downstairs from her room.

"Girls, do you want some lemonade?"

"Yes, please," they replied in unison.

"May I use the bathroom?" Tina asked.

"Of course! You know where it is."

Tina started for the bathroom, but she noticed that, on one side of the hallway, the door to the main room was half open, and she couldn't avoid looking in. She had never seen such strange décor. So black. So macabre.

Crosses and gargoyles lent a very dark ambience to the room. Tina couldn't stand being there, and she never even made it to the bathroom. However, on the floor of the room, there were some newspaper clippings containing news about the arrest of Tina's father. She also saw a photo of the now-accused with four children, among whom was the new girl at school with her red ribbon, Lucecita, and Matt. She couldn't recognize the fourth person, whose face had been scribbled on with red marker. When Tina dropped the photo and turned around, there was Teresa's mother standing right before her with a gun in her hand.

"Ma'am, I was just passing by here and…"

"Don't say anything. Lower your voice, because Lucecita is in Teresa's room," she asked, approaching Tina with a gesture of warning. "I found this today and I'm very upset. That new girl, Lucecita, and Matt, do they know my husband?"

"I don't know what to say. But all that decoration in the room, what's that all about?"

"My husband collects gothic art. I never thought there was anything more to it. Tina, I need you to help me get to the bottom of this."

"Me, Ma'am? How do you suppose I'll be able to do that?"

"Teresa told me she's planning to go camping at the lake on Halloween night. I'm very afraid to let her go but locking her up for her whole life won't help her either. Besides, I want you to watch Lucecita and Matt to see what they're up to. I'll rent a cabin, and you'll stay there with me. You'll say you can't be outside because you have asthma, okay?"

"Yes…yes…But…"

"Nobody will know that I'm there since I'll lock myself in the room. You'll come in only if it's necessary. The girls didn't want to stay in the cabin, so everything will be very safe."

The cold rises from the St. Clair with infinite breaths of cruelty, and at times, the fog permits her to see, though death had made its pronouncement that it was there.

Tina was horrified and didn't understand anything that was going on. She couldn't move. The haze dispersed occasionally, and she was able to observe the ghoulish scene of hundreds of red ribbons floating on the water. At her feet, propelled by the gentle waves of the lake, two rosaries made of human nails polished with fresh blood emerged, making her fall to her knees. She tried to scream. She couldn't.

A final wave dragged Lucecita's broken eyeglasses, with two eyeballs skewered by the black frames that her friend had adjusted so many times to prevent them from falling off.

At the base of the bonfire, a ritual circle, badly drawn in blood and adorned with the heads of several of the students from school, including Matt's. Tina turned to look for help while she tried to take in a mouthful of air. At one corner of the frightful scene lay Father Jim, kneeling and pierced through the throat by a cross.

"Rehtaf Ruo" was written on the hot iron of the cross.

They grabbed Tina very forcefully from behind.

In an effort to escape, she turned her head and saw Teresa, with her hands and mouth bloody.

"Will you come with us to hell, my friend?"

Crow 14

Mortimer's Infidelity

What you don't know is that Mortimer explained his adventures very well, so well that his wife listened attentively to his excuses and, without a trace of recrimination, served him dinner. Or breakfast.

"Darling, you're different from the others, and that's why I fall at your feet, seduced. You're different from the girls who don't understand that we men just want variety. Two butt cheeks. That's all she meant in my life," he says, spraying his drunkenness all around the kitchen.

"It's all right, Mortimer. Let's not talk about it anymore," his wife replied in a way that was as natural as it was bewildering.

It was obvious that that man, who, hours earlier, was frolicking with his secretary in a room of a nameless motel, wasn't prepared for that response. However, he accepted it without qualms, since now, he wouldn't have to work off his exhaustion and the booze on the uncomfortable office couch. If he had to face any kind of discussion, he would do it tomorrow. Yet it wasn't too long before remorse began to prowl around his bedroom, like an unconscious reply to the attention his wife had lavished on him before going to bed. Despite the heaviness of the alcohol, Mortimer chose to spend the night thinking of different scenarios, all of them representing arguments that would forever banish him from his home.

"Mortimer, are you still awake?"

"Yes."

"We need to talk."

"Do you think we can do it tomorrow?"

"Yes, I think it's the most reasonable thing."

121

"Thank you, darling."

"Get some rest. You have a meeting with that important client tomorrow and you need to have a clear mind for that negotiation, which, as you know, will be tough."

"Of course, dear. I had almost forgotten! Damn…"

"Would you like some tea to help you sleep?"

"No, sweetheart. Don't worry so much, please. You're already in bed. You rest."

"It's better if I make you a cup so you can rest and recover for tomorrow."

"No, darling. Don't worry, I insist."

Just as doubts were about to take over his remaining traces of lucidity, Mortimer got out of bed and followed his wife's footsteps.

"What are you doing up? Go to bed…I'll bring you the tea."

"I just wanted to keep you company while you make it," said Mortimer, never taking his eyes off his wife's hands. "You know what? If you want, we can talk now."

"No, honey. You're right. It wouldn't be prudent. You need to get your strength back first. Besides, I need to think about my next step very carefully."

Mortimer felt like he couldn't overcome his doubts. Such indifference following a confessed act of infidelity? Next step? He was able to confirm that the tea was nothing more than that. But now, he'd have to sleep next to his wife. Why hadn't she fallen asleep first? Or was it that thing she had wanted to talk about, which could now wait until tomorrow?

He had made up his mind. He wouldn't sleep that night. No tea could take away such worry. That's why he chose the option of pretending to be asleep, even at the risk of collapsing, exhausted.

They both went to bed. It was 2:39 AM. And the inevitable happened. A fight to the death. But it was a fight between his thoughts and his eyelids, and Mortimer lost that fight. When he opened his eyes again, it was 3:47 AM. He had a hangover, now adding an unbearable headache to the inferno of that early morning hour. Mortimer turned his head to the right and saw his wife's back.

Was it really worth it to cheat on her?

"I'm getting excited!" said his wife without turning around.

"What? Are you awake?"

"It excites me to know that you've been with someone else. That's what I wanted to tell you. I want you to make love to me now and to tell your secretary tomorrow that we should have a threesome. That's what I want."

Mortimer didn't waste one second. The two of them made love like never before. Emotion took over that man, who could think only of how happy his wife's fantasy made him. The next day, there was no important client to rouse him from bed, because after that confession, he would surrender to the deepest sleep, from which, unfortunately, he would never again awaken.

Crow 15

Mima

Havana will always be that place where I want to live because I long for the elegance of its parties, the gold, the banquets, and the pineapple soda of the House of Sarrá. El Morro, El Gran Teatro, or anything else that might make me happy on the Havana Malecón, that historic boardwalk for which the city is famous.

A kiss from Juan Jesús. A theater filled to bursting. An enchanting city in the breeze of the damp rocks, embracing everything it touches, including me. On the other hand, in Villa Blanca, everything is different.

My father is a suntanned, scale-fish fisherman in the northeast of the Pearl of the Antilles. A small, fifteen-foot-long cork boat is all that stands between me, and an accounting certificate earned at the Camagüey Chamber of Commerce. Five cents for high-quality wreckfish, barely enough to provide for our daily pork or squirrelfish. The old man can't waste his sinkers, and opportunity obliges him to fish with his life hanging from every hook.

He risks drowning for our sake and for Mima's, though today is pure happiness: the boat is loaded with catch. The sand on the beach changes shape with the rolling of the waves, concealing my desires, while at the same time, covering any traces left on the beach's surface. A kind of happiness clothed in rags and dreams, cut short by damp stretches of netting, and even though we've always lived this way, I want to go to Havana.

From a distance, we see the cork boat bobbing on the horizon, half out of the water, and Aunt Angela closes the door. The truth? I'm already sick and tired of that old hag.

Whenever party time approaches, she looks me up and down, trying to determine whether Juan Jesús has invited me to the summer carnival contest. Last year, we won second prize, and of course, my father made red snapper with vegetables. That smooth-tongued social climber lost no time in coming out like a dog that's knocked over the pot, carrying an oyster casserole and trying to nose her way around my Juan Jesús. One and one make two, even if she goes rogue, and the story of his romantic escapades is nothing new, as I'm well aware!

In our wooden house at the edge of the saltpeter flats, there's no room for more mouths to feed. Ever since the looters showed up along the coast, Aunt Angela has been going down to the boats with any creep with a half-carafe of rum and a bucket of crabs. Their servile laughter ended up giving her a dry cough, the kind that eventually goes away out of sheer exhaustion.

The old man knows she's screwing around, but he doesn't want to go against Mima. I don't blame him. He also knows he won't eat anymore if he gets into it with his sister-in-law and some fisherman from one of these boats he has to plumb every day.

The looters' nets are very big and drag along any creature that moves through the water. They go around with their big boats, sailing over the vulnerability of smaller crafts and over the fears of those of us who harvest our food from the sea. Then they want to come and sell us tilapia, as if they had caught it off the islands of Japan. Thank God today is different.

For three weeks, the old man has been bringing in less than half a boatload, and there are five of us at home. Mima and I went for a walk over to the Suárez house and picked up the damaged nets to make the rope hammocks that would later be sold at the carnival. A hard job whenever the sheets of netting get tangled in whatever the fishermen throw back. Beside the hunger and frustration of those who live along the coast, the hardest thing to deal with is a forgotten net.

Alvarito, my older brother, goes out with my dad whenever they let him, because Mima told him to look for a school in the capital. He's the one chosen for book learning because, according to Mima, I ought to marry Juan Jesús. And finally, there's Aunt Angela, that old hag, who cleans hotels in the area, besides cleaning the pockets of tourists along the way.

If only Saint Lazarus would work a miracle and let me marry Juan Jesús!

A good man, outgoing, with a dream of setting up a fast-food place beneath the burning sun of Gibara.

The group, El Tres de Matamoros, makes its way through the alleys of Villa Blanca, while I find work as an assistant at the drugstore. The TB patients show up looking for calcium, which brings in twenty dollars a shot for Barbarito, the druggist. I've seen how he sticks in the needle. Soon, I'll start charging ten. Barbarito watches me. He teaches me. I can charge fifteen.

In two months, I'll take my exam at the Chamber of Commerce. Luis, Juan Jesús' dad, has a contact at the Bank of Camagüey. If I pass the exam, I'll work there as a bookkeeper, even if Juan Jesús insists on setting up his fast-food place.

Accounts payable, accounts receivable, capital. Bonds, debt, and interest.

The nights go by, in the wake of numbers that the cork boats, toasted by the sea, will never understand. Mima prepares the coffee thermos, and Aunt Angela takes advantage of my empty room to soak her feet. Juan Jesús is thinking about me. I feel it in the tickle at the back of my neck and in Aunt Angela's rage, like a jealous dog.

That woman ought to know I'm not made of steel. The women in Villa Blanca are hot to trot, even the overripe ones, damned if they aren't! You can smell experience on their skin. I don't want to fall into temptation, but the last time I paid a call on Rosita, that shameless slut winked at me. What a crazy thing—just imagine—and she's a relative, too!

Rosita has this idea of going to Camagüey to work with numbers, and that's not my thing. I do very well selling engine gaskets. We make the gaskets from the materials we gather at the cookie company and the train station. The cookie company, La Paloma del Castillo, belongs to a Galician, who's been on the island for a long time. My brother-in-law, Alvarito, sneaks the cookie tins out, and we chip them with a hammer and chisel to turn them into a sheet of smooth tin. Then comes the asbestos, which we steal from the railroad station on weekend nights, when the guards get drunk on cheap rum and made-up songs.

Tin, asbestos, and tin. Tin, asbestos, and tin. They sell for thirty dollars apiece. When we run out of asbestos, we offer them out of cardboard. They can't get wet, but they last up to three months. How many numbers do you need for that? But Rosita doesn't understand.

And that's what life is like in Fulgencio Batista's Cuba, because things are too tough to be thinking about El Banco de Camagüey! Luckily, there are already rumors of revolution on the mountainsides. Things have to change, and I'm going to set up my fast-food place in Gibara, you know—fried tilapia with sweet potato! That rocks, man!

At this time of night, there are no buses. But Chichi owes me two gaskets, and I'm gonna ask him for a lift to Rosita's house. I imagine they're asleep, and I'd better get over there before the old man turns the motor over. It's one in the morning, and the lights are already out. I throw a little stone at the bedroom window so the old lady will come out. I've brought along a blanket and a half-full bottle of Paticruzado rum.

The shameless old broad climbs out the window. I hope Rosita won't notice.

I fell asleep on top of the book; numbers didn't add up.

I'll never pass the test this way. I heard a strange noise outside the house. The old man's asleep, too, and I don't wanna wake him over what was probably Nina's dog barking. Nina's our neighbor from the Bruzual house. I lift my cheek from the old dining room table. The lines in the wood have left marks on my face. I remove the padlock from the brass door. There's not much light outside, and I walk slowly to avoid waking anyone. It's full-on night now, and the sea has its own rhythm. The makeshift dock watches me, as if asking me to stay away from a danger I'm unable to notice.

I glance at the cork boat and see that it's moving in a strange way because the waves are going in a different direction. I have to call the old man!

The stench of cheap rum suggests the presence of a drunk. I carefully draw near, and with my right hand, I pick up a grubby blanket.

Mima! Why you? And with Juan Jesús?

Crow 16

On the Shores of the Guatavita

She leaves her shining palace and emerges from the lake to meet Zipa. Her daughter walks alongside her, eyes closed. The raft stops and the ceremony begins. Standing beneath the rays of the sun, impressive and with his back toward the tribe, the yellow man silences the dancing voices of the drunks who accuse that woman of infidelity, and the priest's voice, as well. Among thick shrubs surrounded by cloistered greenery, the gods observe the tension of the ritual, Zipa's raised arms, and the girl's closed eyes, which continue to distill the crystal-clear waters of Lake Guatavita.

Shadow, and then light. The golden dust piled on Zipa's hands is the sign of the offering that the woman doesn't want to receive.

The priest steps back and she approaches.

His arms more and more agitated, Zipa tries to kneel at the feet of his family, returned to him by the water, but the pride of being the Great Chieftain does not allow this. He raises his eyes toward the sun, while spilling the golden powder on the surface of the lake, like someone who spills all hope of being pardoned. From the raft come golden offerings in an attempt to compensate Pachamama and make her merciful in the eyes of the *muiscas*. With her daughter in her arms, the woman's expressionless face looks up at the outcry of those present, those absent, and even of Zipa.

"This is your daughter!" the woman utters with a heart-rending shout that echoes in the depths of the Guatavita, while at the same time, she vanishes, pointing to the priest.

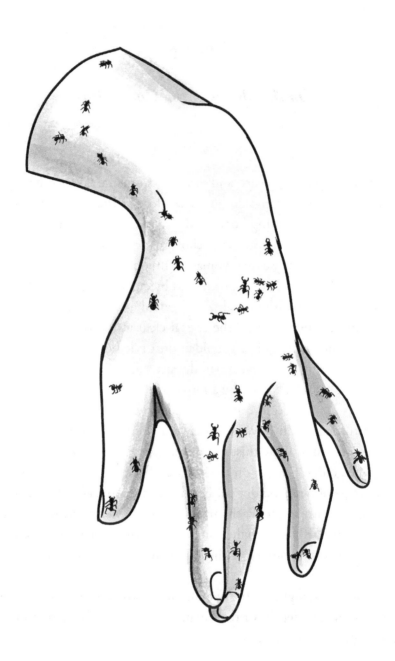

Crow 17

Feromondo

A terrible headache makes me beg for a little more time.

My first steps of the day arrive, accompanied by a coffee, my email, and my schedule, in that order. Outside the tent, two members of the excavation team chatter endlessly. They come from the coast, and they don't understand our slang. Besides, I realize that I have no clean clothes and search for some in my luggage. I put on the ones from yesterday. The laptop is very slow. Maybe it's time to buy a new one. I'll have to wait for the economy to improve.

"Dr. Restrepo, come here. You need to see this!" exclaims one of the assistants.

I step outside the tent and see a great deal of activity all around me. Just a few minutes ago, I was considering the possibility of taking the day off, though I now see that it will prove impossible.

"There's nothing to suggest that I can escape this important find," I think, ironically, just as Pablo, one of the interns under my supervision, approaches.

"Well, it seems like we've got something very interesting. I've followed the trail of the archeological peaks of Cartagena for more than a decade, and I've never seen anything like this," I remark to Pablo.

My name is Gilberto Restrepo and I'm an archeologist at the University of Michigan. Today, I find myself squatting here with a brush fearfully clutched in my right hand, digging a stone plaque out from beneath the base of an almond tree. With my left hand, I pick up my tape recorder and turn it on to give evidence of the registry.

Monday, June 31, 1995. Time: 8:25 AM. I read the inscription on
the plaque:

> I lift my hands as I fall destroyed at the feet of his halberd.
> This does not mean that I am wounded, but that you
> are unharmed. Memory punishes me, while time runs
> against me.
> F.L., 1806

Intoxicated before the splendor of the discovery and with scrupulous
scientific rigor, I order the excavation team to proceed with the extraction
of the plaque, as well as to begin its transfer for further analysis, not
without first noting that the emerging tomb is in a vertical position.

Could it have been a lack of space due to some sort of epidemic during
the colonial period? And if it was, why didn't they build mass graves?

My doubts, the smell of damp earth, and adrenaline invade my
thoughts, converting them into a sigh of indispensable ecstasy at the
base of that almond tree. I believe I know what I have before my eyes,
though unconsciously, I refuse to trust its worth. I plan to put away the
tape recorder, and I signal to Pablo to keep digging all the way to the
bottom. My hunch is even stronger. My desire to run away and abandon
the scene mix with an urgency to remain there, motionless, astonished,
imperturbable. I'm frozen by an insolent expectation that paralyzes
everything. All around me is a mysterious hole, Pablo's muddy hands,
and my frightful headache.

However, and against all predictions, inside the cavity there is no
evidence whatsoever of human remains. Instead, there is a small, skin-
covered manuscript, as well as a few wicker rods, some soot, and ashes.
On the cover, aged from its obvious confinement, a mysterious title
written in italics emerges: *Feromondo*.

"Doctor, what is this?" Pablo inquires uneasily.

"Please, safeguard it immediately! This, my dear Pablo, might be
the Holy Grail of Cartagena's colonial history," I reply, withdrawing
to my tent.

Pablo agrees, his hopes placed on what I am unable to tell him and also in the face of what might be a stroke of luck for our diminished archeological reputation. For the time being, the sun doesn't want to come out. It refuses to grant us the day we need in order to continue, and so, at the imminence of the impertinent rain, we are forced to call off the excavations. We gather our tents, cordoning off the area, and we climb into our all-terrain vehicle. Nelson and Nidia, two members of the team, will remain in the tow truck to protect the discovery zone. Pablo and I want to get back to the lab as soon as possible.

Back at the lab, anxiety tries to drive me over the edge. I ask Pablo to prepare a worktable while I finish gobbling an arepa left over from yesterday that will serve as my impromptu meal. I respect the isolation protocol to avoid contaminating the piece, and I turn on the lamps. I pick up the calipers. My pulse racing with emotion and logic, I try very cautiously to separate the first pages, aged by time, and painted sporadically with erratic rings of humidity. Then, I begin reading aloud:

> I come with the horde that is defending the reed bed, and I cannot recognize my own body, nor that of the other man, who is nearby and not even in the other one over there whom I cannot smell. I walk between the cracks of the unattainable, through which my dark body moves roughly in the presence of another soldier, who invites me to elude him with an almost reverent salute. A few spaces away, the lifeless seeds are raffled off for the most battle-hardened.
>
> The larva of the fruit orchards, now stripped bare by the bloodthirsty jaws, serve as an aperitif for the funeral procession that will carry it to its final home. I stop before the almond tree, and everyone behind me does the same. I clean my nose to protect it from all the confusion. I wait for the larva's funereal passage, while at the same time, marking the cranberry seed behind the dry moss.
>
> The larva's remains carry me back to another time when I was what I no longer am, and when I witnessed so many

135

funeral processions promoted by the dogmatic ignorance of a few, because the larva dies to feed our bodies, while the accused die to feed our differences. The larva dies because of our social organization. In the world of heresies, the marked ones die to justify the unjustifiable.

Within this memory, now extracted by the damp, fallen leaves, there emerges my own memory of the month of March in the year 1741 in Cartagena de Indias, the ancient lands of the Calamares, Caribes, and countless others. Within this doubt-riddled memory, we defended ourselves from the infamous attack by beings with unusual eyes, who had retreated before the ferocity of our soldiers, and who now found themselves hiding in secluded places, hidden behind the pond that provided our food, but which also brought us death. Within this memory, colored by the multitude that today surrounds my domain, abides the hope of organizing ourselves in strange and asynchronous types of battle. Within this memory, far from my Feromondo, our orders were implacable and skin color had a different value, both for the vice regency and for the barbarians and their iron crosses.

I was a giant, endowed with two arms, two legs, two eyes, and a special way of stridulating. I didn't live as I do now, in underground galleries, invisible to the incalculably huge meteorites or the terrible, winged steamrollers suspended from the sky. However, I lived imprisoned by my own interests, by the inequality imposed by the European crown through the House of Bourbon and the other dreamlike beliefs of the Court of the Inquisition of Cartagena.

I no longer understand.

Now, the passage obstructed by the festival of the fallen larva has been restored, while I advance, along with the rhythm of the others, in directions marked by those who have gone before me. The strong odor of the Feromondo summons us to repel attacks by other beings, also those with unusual eyes. Their numbers are legion.

The odor of the signal forces us to organize almost instantly, so as to impede the brazen intruders' attack. Perhaps, today, I will die among stingers desperate for bits of food or beneath sharp halberds that will destroy me, but which will also inject me with large doses of satisfaction in the light of just causes. The monster standing before me is twice my size and advances fiercely, though I am swifter. I try to grip him in order to sting his magnificence. The effort fails, and my body, exposed to the furious counterattack, capsizes in the rigor of the battle. In the end, our accumulated dead, piled up at the entrance to the colony, will prevent them from getting in.

I raise my hands as I fall, destroyed, at the feet of his halberd. This does not mean I am wounded, but rather that neither are you. Memory punishes me, while time flows against me.

F.L., 1806

"What does all this mean?" Pablo asks,

"It's about the Legend of the Feromondo!" I reply, panting at the excitement of the moment.

"Feromondo?"

"According to the legend, during the Colonial period—dominated by the Viceregency and by the Holy Inquisition of the Catholic Church—a soldier named Federico Luján was accused of heresy and condemned to terrible torture."

"Federico was buried standing in such a way that only his head and shoulders were visible to the hangmen. Then, they sprinkled drops of honey and musk on his forehead, every three seconds, at the base of an almond tree. The punishment was opened to the public so as to show people, especially the soldiers of the Viceregency, what awaited all those who defied the political and ecclesiastical authority of Nueva Granada. Despite the uproar and the desperate screams of the hapless soldier, he was not pardoned by the Holy Office, but rather was slowly devoured by colonies of ants, leading to a painful death. His body was buried in the same place where he was murdered, and the settlers say that Federico's suffering fell upon thousands of uttered curses, while his wandering soul was able to possess the body of an ant. Federico would remain a soldier, but in a different body. He would rest in peace only when the Holy Inquisition was abolished, which, in theory, took place in the year 1811, with the expulsion of the Spaniards. The legend was never proved, but we now have in our hands a document that could change history."

"This is incredible," said Pablo, holding his head in his hands.

I now have irrefutable evidence that will lay to rest many theories about the Legend of the Feromondo. However, the call I received just minutes later would change the course of events. The archeological dig zone around the almond tree has disappeared, and the area around it has been colonized by a nest of enormous ants.

Crow 18

Olivia and Me

How many cars have gone by since I woke up?

Maybe thirty. Nuki wouldn't believe that there were so few. At best, he might have earned a few cans, but it's better he's gone off to some corner far from here with his stories of other lives.

The juggler steals all the attention, but, as always, the others have done a very good job of concealing that. They watch with great concentration while he picks up the flaming rods, but they immediately redirect their eyes to the horizon with an indifference colored by a bad mood.

With the juggler? Not with him, I can't, because he hits very hard. On the other hand, with Nuki maybe, if he can manage to remain standing. Of course, he owes me three boxes, but I know where to find him. The traffic light turns red, though the circus heeds the green of assumed liberties. The first to arrive is a young man in a little white car. He rolls up the window even though I'm not looking at him. I hardly ever do. The others don't like it, and they hit very hard, too. In the vehicle next to that one is a widow with her son, who's licking candy in the back seat of their red van.

"That man is dirty, Mama! Scold him!" he says, rolling down the window and pointing at me with his strange, little finger.

The widow watches me. I keep ignoring her and picking up the boxes. I know she's a widow because she's dressed in black and today, she didn't comb her hair. Now, she tells her son to keep quiet and to roll up the window. The boy doesn't obey and keeps pointing at me, while his candy falls to the unforgiving sidewalk. The same sidewalk I walk every day, nearly barefoot, to escape the juggler or to collect a few pennies.

"Where's Olivia?" I ask, looking down at the ground.

I see her, turn around, and walk toward her.

Haven't we all been forgotten at some point? I ask myself, my thoughts wandering.

Behind me, and at the edge of the sidewalk, Olivia is frozen, exactly where I left her last night. It's a good sign of the territorial truce with the juggler, since he tends to hide her when he wants me to go away.

With these two cars, there must already be around thirty-two, I think, rearranging Olivia's bags. I count the cans. The cloths from the drugstore aren't all the same color. The same thing happens with the old newspapers I collect to learn about the world after the fact. Actually, I'm waiting for the juggler to do his thing, for the traffic light to change, and for the boy to stop staring at me. As for the candy, I couldn't care less.

I still need a few cans for Lorenzo to give me what I'm after, but in the no-man's-land where Olivia is resting, there are only bags, empty bottles from the ones Lorenzo gives me, and other things that are only good for throwing at the stray dogs that want to sprawl out on my boxes. Inside Olivia there are enough bags. I call her Olivia because I brought her home from that supermarket. The left front wheel is all messed up, loose, but Nuki put in a clothes hanger that will hold her in place as long as I don't push her very hard. Or at least that's what that crooked can thief told me, so I'd give him a sip of the half bottle of rum I had left.

My belly is rumbling because I haven't seen Lorenzo in two days. I need a hundred cans, and I have ninety-something. The traffic light changes. The young man in the white car hits the gas impulsively, and the widow gets away from the situation, as uncomfortable for her as it is for me. I turn around and stow the boxes. I make sure all the vehicles have gone. The juggler crosses the avenue, heading for the opposite corner; this time, uttering curses that make me think that at some point, he'll come for me.

I hope he gets what he's looking for, because if he doesn't, he'll want to take Olivia away again, and nobody messes with Olivia. With Nuki, maybe, but with Olivia, no.

On that same side and to the right of the juggler lives the jumpy girl with the dog. Every day, she walks around taking little leaps of happiness in the crosswalk toward my corner and the drugstore, and I have to hide behind Olivia because the dog barks at me and the girl can't hold on to him for very long.

The juggler laughs, and I throw trash at him. It's the start of a battle that I always lose, and then I have to find a place to sleep somewhere else. With Nuki, it was easier to frighten the dog, but I had to share my cans, Lorenzo's bottles, the boxes, and the scornful looks with her, and even the juggler's blows.

There are hardly any passersby on my sidewalk since they all avoid me from one block back. It's better that way. They never give me anything, and when they greet me, they do it by shaking their heads "no." The different ones have those strange ways of showing contempt.

I scratch my right leg wherever the torn pants allow me to. The sun speeds up its race through time, and I curl up on top of the boxes. I always talk to myself, and I even have arguments with myself. I do it so that the others will know I'm here and that this is my corner—the only thing I own beside Olivia, the cans, the old newspapers where they sell worlds of poetry, and the boxes.

I have to get my hands on more cans, and I know it. But the grumpy old guy who lives next door to the girl with the dog hasn't taken out the trash yet. He usually does it just as the sun grows bigger above my boxes and the congestion clutters up the traffic light. Sometimes, he leaves something to snack on in front of Lorenzo's bottles. Last week, I snagged a pair of shoes that burned me less than these, but the juggler took them from me. I stole three balls from him—the kind he throws into the air—and I exchanged them with Nuki for a partly-nibbled pizza that he found at the gas station on the other street.

The juggler thinks it was the little girl's dog. He said he was going to poison it.

Poor little girl—to have to contend with the juggler, too. But it's not too much to hope that the barking beast will disappear in the child's forgetfulness.

The light changes again and marks my life on top of the boxes. I gather them up, I turn around, I check Olivia, I run away from the dog, and I count the vehicles to make a bet with Nuki when he shows up, but everything seems to suggest he won't come today, which means that that terrible opportunist has worked out some kind of swap with Lorenzo. This time, three cars have come up to the traffic light, two yellow ones, and the other silver. In the first row, a yellow coupe with a stretched-out lady who's looking at herself in the rearview mirror as she talks to him.

"The others are strange…they talk to themselves, too!" I tell Olivia.

I imagine she's doing it to frighten off the juggler. Beside them, a man in a hat in a classic minivan with his arm resting on top of the door. I hope he'll let go of the tobacco he's holding in his hand.

When I was one of them, I liked tobacco, too. Now, I don't because it burns my gums when I drink. But it would be better to get that tobacco in case I don't collect all the cans.

I look at the minivan from the corner of my eye and wave to the smoker, who's looking in a different direction, and at the same time, I talk to myself about the almost non-existent possibility that the tobacco might fall onto the sidewalk.

Behind those two is a yellow pick-up truck loaded with all sorts of trash, from an enormous leather sofa to aluminum rods of all sizes, not even counting the multi-colored boxes. One minute in the pick-up with Olivia and I get Lorenzo to give me all the bottles for the week.

The passenger in the pick-up is a youngster, around thirteen years old; he rolls up the window and stares at me attentively. I'm used to it, and I continue to look at the man in the minivan ahead of him. The youngster talks to the driver beside him and decides to roll down the window. With a gesture that I almost never see among them, he asks me to come closer. I look in all directions, and the juggler tries to get to the pick-up before me. The driver tells him to go away, and I feel uneasy. The youngster calls me over again, and this time, I approach the vehicle.

He gives me a cold can with some nasty liquid in it!

Avoiding eye contact with him, I take it and run off. He rolls up his window again, and the driver gives him a hug. From the other corner, the juggler watches me and looks in his box of balls for the shoes he stole from me. He shows them to me.

No way am I about to give him the can! He threatens me with his fist. In the end, all of us are the way I was with Nuki. I open the can quickly and spill out the nasty liquid on Olivia's wheels. Then, I stand it up on the sidewalk and step on it with the worn-out sole of my left shoe, the foot that causes me the least pain when I walk. But anger is pouring out of me from every corner of my mind, since I ought to have the shoes that the grumpy old guy left in the dump, which the heartless juggler wants to swap me for the only thing I'll have this week: a bottle of rum from Lorenzo's liquor store.

The kid in the pick-up cries desperately because I spilled the liquid. The driver hugs him. Then, he gets out of the pick-up and insults me in a thousand different ways.

Now, from the other street, the jumpy girl with the dog appears and waits for the pedestrian crossing sign. I decide to stay behind Olivia.

Three threats at the same traffic light, and I'm still short a few cans. I take Olivia because I know it's time for me to move on.

I'll give Nuki a can in exchange for spending one day on his block.

Crow 19

An Afternoon in Cayapán

The tree wasn't there last year, when I came to Cayapán in search of melons and adventures with women. I also came for a little liquor to ward off the November cold. I carry it with me, four or five bottles at a time. It depends on the cost of the barrels. Sometimes, the vendors see my lucky expression and ask for as much as sixty bucks, but I'm not really a lucky guy at all. I'm more of a bargainer and live wire.

The trip across the mountain is long, and the horses go wherever they want. On the way there, they go at a trot; they like the inn. And on the way back, well, that's when things change. That's why I tie them up in the shade so that they can eat, drink, and rest from the heat. The road is rocky and not made for any old horseshoes. Silvio González, the town blacksmith, charges me twenty bucks, which means a total of one-hundred twenty, including my canteen. After 6:00 PM and fully loaded, the return trip is kind of hard. Well, not really hard. What happens is that poor devils like me can't allow themselves the luxury of being robbed by the Sifontes gang. The problem isn't the sixty bucks for the booze. No, Sir. It's the horses, the rifle, and the wagon. Ah, and life, too, because in San Jacinto, they say that they don't like to leave anybody breathing. That's why I hardly ever come to Cayapán. I don't like to cross the mountains. The boys don't, either, because when we get there, the dapple-gray looks like he's begging for the wild horses' grassland, while the other one, the spotted sorrel, doesn't even lift his head from the trough.

Cayapán is dry from the get-go. It's like a blessing to find water for the horses. It seems like an invisible line marks the place where the mountains end, giving way to a blazing inferno. I think the sun hates that town. After the smallest hills welcome you in the afternoon, you have to say hello to the young flower vendors. Don't run away; it's one buck for the offering to San Miguel de Cayapán. It's expensive, yes. One buck for white carnations that grow in the mountains, to place them on the altar at the inn, right there, where you pass the entrance sign, to the right.

On one side it says, "Welcome to Cay pán." It looks like the letter "a" fell off or maybe it was erased out of revenge. "Thank you for your visit," says the other side. I don't know why it says that, because nobody comes to visit here; in fact, coming to Cayapán is a favor. Maybe they put it there for the mezcal dealers to see when they come loaded with hearts of agave and melons from the harvest. They sell and they go, with short mouthfuls and long reins. You can't see all their faces because they know that their hats were made to cover them. That's how they wear sombreros here: halfway down their noses and with their throats exposed. Of those cart drivers, three take care of business at the cantinas, half the town. The rest don't leave the fields to come to Cayapán unless they're skirt-hunters. Looking for girls, I mean. Those skirts always change everything, just like the rest area at the entrance to town changes the way the colts whinny. But don't even think of going in without making an offering.

Some say that San Miguel de Cayapán will mark you with its scorn. I say that the young flower vendors pass on the information to the Sifontes. Whatever, it's not a good idea to go by without greeting the saint. Ah, they charge you five bucks for the rest area. That makes six. Add that, if you will, to the one hundred fifty we had, because I always leave the other one hundred twenty for the skirts.

As if that weren't enough, the horses always stand up straight when we go down the hill to the Río Santo, and they prick up their ears like a couple of those antennas that come with appliances from the city. They also pick up their pace to greet the sun, but I'm sure they wonder where that tree came from. And you see, like I said, it wasn't there last year. It popped up suddenly and it's about fifteen feet tall, not exactly little, either. I probably saw it last year when I arrived all drowsy from listening to Agapito's stories. Or could it be that I was overcome by drowsiness and my eyelashes kept falling off?

Agapito didn't come. Not this time. It's a business opportunity, but at the same time, it doesn't do me any good. He pays me twenty bucks for the ride, but he talks a lot and I fall asleep. Oh, and he drinks my booze. Those twenty bucks could help me cover the cost of the trip, which is one hundred seventy, because my wife asked me to bring her some melons from San Jacinto. They really have a lot of those. The melons, and everything in general that they grow there, are of good quality. But that's where the Sifontes are from, and the toll is very expensive.

Around thirty wagons on, I see the inn with that new tree. Some colts surround it—not many. When I take off my hat, I can see maybe three of them from here. Maybe they moved them, I mean, for the horses. It's a mango tree. I pull it out by the leaves, and if I know anything, it's full of mangos. Aunt Berta had two of those trees on her porch. I used to pass by in the afternoon, splashing around in the damp earth with the soles of my shoes whenever I returned from the country school, where they taught me to use a pencil. I would sit at the foot of the biggest tree and knock down the mangos with Uncle Julio's stick so that I could eat them sprinkled with pepper in January. Then, I really plucked them out of the ground. When I got home, an hour later, my feet were full of mud and my mouth was all sticky from so many loose threads, but at least I had eaten. But not just mango. No, Sir. Because Aunt Berta kept me away from the pig or the chickens, and I did my homework right there.

Uncle Julio also taught me to ride. Those are all the things you need to do at that age in La Arboleda del Paso. Well, that and also the thing with the donkeys, but that's none of your business.

When I got home, Mom was waiting for me with the daily chores, like bringing water from the well, or cutting the straw on the patio with a machete that couldn't take any more grinding. My hands moved all by themselves from pulling on the casing so much. I would watch the wagons coming along the path and the donkeys loaded with corn and all kinds of seeds on their way to Cayapán to be sold or exchanged for liquor. I heard the dry creaking of the wagons against the stones and the tapping of the luckiest ones, who went on horseback.

Someday, I'll have my own wagon with two chestnut horses, because those give birth to lots of foals and cost more, I thought with each blow of the machete against the wreaths of moss.

"Good money for the rides," I said to Uncle Julio.

Every three weeks, between March and September, the mares started to act strange. In any case, it had something to do with the mangos, because there were always mangos—well, almost always. That's how I know that the tree over there is a mango tree.

"Listen, child, give me a branch for San Miguel…"

"Three dollars."

"Three bucks…Girl, this one cost one buck, right?"

"Today is San Miguel's day…"

"San Miguel…Oh, damn. Look, sweetheart, what about that mango tree by the rest stop?"

"The mayor planted that one."

"The mayor…What do you charge for a quickie?"

"You'll have to ask at the bar…"

"At the bar… Okay, fine. I see it over there, past the rest stop… Giddyup!"

Getting there's no big deal. What's harder is struggling with the dapple-gray to keep him from pulling to the right. There aren't many working rest stops along the road, I mean, enough to take it all calmly. Around here, two donkey riders set out, for San Jacinto, say, or maybe a little closer by, like Portabales, a hamlet with only ten families on the other side of the Río Santo. At least it seems like that's where they go because the donkeys look like they're in good shape. I nod, tipping my hat, and I keep going, following the whim of the dapple-gray.

"Where are you coming from?" asks the park attendant.

"Where am I coming from? From La Arboleda…"

"That'll be ten bucks."

"Ten bucks…Okay…Didn't it cost five?"

"It's because of San Miguel's day and for the mango."

"For the mango…Ah…Now, I see where the business of the mango comes from. I've got eight…You're not going to keep me out for two bucks! Besides, the flower girl already took three bucks from me."

"Are you new around here?"

"New around here? No, I'm Loreto, Agapito's cousin. From the vegetable vendors."

"Oh, yeah! Agapito. Go on in, please. You owe me two bucks."

"Two bucks, okay. Well, we'll work this out on my next trip. Giddyup!"

At the rest stop, I notice that they accept cruppers and that they have more watering troughs.

A young kid, around eleven years old, with sleeves worn out by labor and a little hat that doesn't really fit him, is picking up manure with a whisk broom from plowing, whose pole has been cut off. That way, he can bend over more easily to deposit it into the harvest bag. The kid says that it's so that it won't stick to the wagon wheels. I think he wants to use it for compost. The dapple-gray is annoying me. I make way for him. The kid with the manure stretches the brim of his hat downward because he has other intentions.

"Whatever you'd like to pay…" says the kid, tears in his eyes.

"Like to pay? Don't they pay you at the rest stop?"

"Half a buck for five bags of manure."

"Five bags of manure…and where do you live?"

"Behind the Río Santo, where it forks to the left."

"To the left…That's Portabales…"

"Yes, Sir…"

"Why don't you sell the manure in the fields? They'll give you a little more there."

"Sir, the manure belongs to the caretaker at the rest stop."

"To the caretaker…Well, I'm going to give you half a buck, but take care of my horses."

"Whatever you say, Sir," replies the boy, his eyes brimming with happiness.

After chatting with the kid and helping my horses settle in, I collect the bag with the two hundred bucks from the seat of the wagon and check to see what's inside. Ah…And the flowers. I walk about thirty steps toward the exit from the rest stop. There is the altar to San Miguel. I pray very quietly because I don't know how to pray, but mostly, so people will see me. Amen. I bend my head in a sign of reverence, with my hat on my chest, and I go to check on the donkeys. No, Sir. I'm not going to walk all the way over to the bar because it's half the town's length away, and after two hours in the wagon, my knees are cramping. There are some animals available for twenty bucks a day with saddle, and ten without.

"Sweetie, aren't you the girl who sells flowers?"

"Yes, but I also handle the business with the donkeys."

"Ah. The business with the donkeys…Look, I'll give you seven bucks for the smallest one, no saddle."

"No, Sir. They cost twenty for riding bareback."

"Twenty for bareback. Because it's San Miguel's day, right?"

"Yes. Now you understand me."

"She understands me. Yes. That donkey looks kind of worn out. I don't think anybody will want to take him. Let's make it ten and we'll meet over there in the room."

"Fifteen, Sir, and bring him back to me early."

"Early, fine. I've only got twelve. I hadn't counted on those three bucks for the flowers, plus ten for the rest stop, and the kid who collects manure. Little girl, as you'll surely understand, in La Arboleda, all we sell is corn."

"Twelve…Okay, that's fine. But don't bring him back to me here. You can return him to me at the bar."

"At the bar? No way. Little girl, I'd rather walk."

"You weigh less than seventy kilos without your hat, and I'm light. We'll go together."

"We'll go together…That really changes things…All right, take the ten."

"It's twelve."

"Twelve...All right...We'll work it out on the way back. Giddyup!"

The hung-over donkey doesn't walk because of the furrows left by the wagons; instead, he clings to the sides, and it's tougher like that. From the entrance to the bar, you can see houses, vegetable vendors, fields, and all sorts of repair places. They repair this and that. When you live in these towns, you've got to buy life from objects. Saddlers, carpenters, blacksmiths, and even folk healers. They repair the years on you. Or like Agapito's slick helper, who sells you whatever the fields cast off. That clever fox fixes your hunger. Misshapen tomatoes, potatoes with holes in them, toasted onions, and melons that look like they were squashed by the mushrooms clinging to their roots. They sell them by the bag, which turns out to be cheaper. The bag of "spoiled stuff," as it's called, sells at two for five bucks, and he carries it back to your house. You salvage half the contents, and the rest is for the animals.

On the way back from the cornfield, old man Aponte's land begins. Acres and acres of fertile soil, so vast that you can't see where they end. A white point beneath the mountain marks the old man's ranch. He lives there with two of his children because the old lady hanged herself with a rope and the oldest daughter became an artist. She moved away to the city, though around here, people say she left because she liked to paint naked women. Well, anyway, that's what they say in the town.

Now, just a few steps from the bar, everything looks closed. From outside, you can always see the men gathered in the fresh air, but not today, no, Sir. It doesn't really look like they were celebrating San Miguel's day at all. I think the heat scared them off because they left some of their horses outside—maybe five of them—all chestnuts, pedigreed. Some big shot must have come to Cayapán, because you don't see fine animals like those too often around here.

I tie up the donkey right there, close at hand. "Cayapán Cantina" reads the wooden sign in white paint, to make the name stand out. Once the donkey had been safely tethered, I dry my forehead with a towel I've brought from the wagon and put my hat back on. This time, I glance all around. I pick up the flask and drink because the drowsiness is extreme,

153

and the stones on the ground are boiling. I've got the bag with the three hundred bucks tied to my belt with a cord. But that bag is resting in my pocket so that no one will know that I'm carrying three hundred fifty right there. As you know, the little flower vendor is coming later to pick out the room and collect the donkey. I draw back the curtain and see all of that lying on the ground.

"I'll be damned! So, now, people pray to San Miguel while lying on the ground?"

"Hands up, you starving bastard, and get down on the floor. We're the Sifontes gang!"

Imagine how my hands trembled when I saw that gunman aiming at my hat.

"The Sifontes…Yes. Don't rush me. I come in peace."

"Where's the bag?" asks the short guy with a long, gray beard and a short rifle.

"The bag…What bag?" I reply.

"The one with one hundred fifty bucks in it! I mean, the little one you've got in your pocket."

"The little red one in my pocket…Okay, all right. Take it however you like!"

After sacking the bar, the Sifontes gang left the bar like a soul carried off by the devil, firing several shots into the air.

"Loreto!" shouts the barkeeper. "If you'd gotten here a minute later, you wouldn't have lost your one hundred fifty bucks."

"One hundred and fifty bucks…No, they took twenty. The ones I had saved for the room."

"Twenty? So, why did you say you had more?"

"That I had more? No, Sir. What happened is that they don't raise idiots in La Arboleda. And as far as I know, Cayapán doesn't even have a mayor, and the little flower vendor doesn't make enough to buy donkeys."

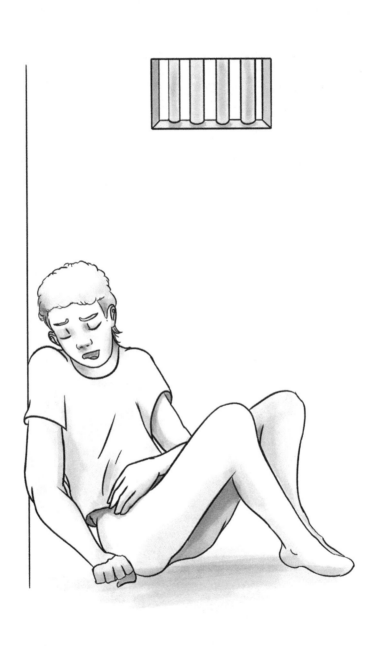

Crow 20

Between Two Moons, Your Eyes

The view isn't impressive, but at least the window is still there.

Four bars, consumed by waiting, try to tell me stories of a time that, walking on my back, disappears at the count of four. The bar at the extreme left of the blue eyes is the same one I squeeze with the fingers of my right hand. Two realities separated by metal. Two lives separated by the same discovered desires. From the ceiling, worn out by so much humidity, a hesitant drip slides down, attempting to explain this vulnerability.

"Will the eyes appear today?" I wonder, confused.

The vulnerability I'm telling you about is the only thing I've had to embrace. The bars might change position, pair off, or even disappear, but their shadows will continue to be projected in a rhythm marked by the sweet melody of the impatient light. After all, what the light decides to do with them doesn't interest me.

Seen through the halo are Juan, Ana, Pilar, and Casimiro. That's what I decided to call the four bars that dance on the cold concrete where my naked feet, infinitely dying, lie. I said it didn't interest me, though my great secret is that when Juan decides to have sex with Ana, Pilar and Casimiro hide, embarrassed by the gaze of those eyes that come from outside, or from inside, or from nowhere, or from hope, or from a world that I now keep forever.

All I know is that in the glimmering darkness, Juan will send the moon to Casimiro, like at the madman's funeral procession. Ana and Pilar will be able to reach it only partially, while Casimiro waits crouching, with marks carved by the sweat of my fingers. All this happens only if the mischievous moon doesn't hide so that Juan will leave Ana alone. The moon knows that Pilar will never surrender to Casimiro while she is watching, and that I will be there to watch over her departure through the leafiness of the trees that reveal themselves from treetop to treetop and in the midst of which the blue eyes will emerge to give me one more day of newly fragrances.

Stationed before such imminent emotion, the blue eyes break through, their stems pointing downward and their multicolored petals blending in with the blue sky. They cling to any tree that will allow itself to be embraced, and they greet me, despite Juan and Ana's indecency. Those two orchids came again today to visit me. I will keep waiting for Pilar and Casimiro to leave, as if they were searching for one another on their own voyage. A voyage that will never be completed, of course, until the next moon decides never to appear again.

Crow 21

Flight 1039

"Passengers for Bloowish Airlines Flight 1039 to Oslo, please proceed to Gate Three."

"Second call: Passengers for Bloowish Airlines Flight 1039 to Oslo, please proceed to Gate Three."

Despite how strange I find this situation, and after checking the outrageous price of a bottle of Paco Rabanne at the Anchorage International Duty-Free Shop, I head for the boarding gate. I pick up my fur coat. I throw away my recently purchased cup of coffee and look around, perplexed.

"Good morning, Miss. Is this the flight to Oslo?" I ask the pleasant blonde at the gate, handing her my passport and boarding pass.

"Good morning, Mr…um…Larsson," she replies, checking my ticket. "Yes, welcome aboard. Just follow this corridor and the flight attendant will show you to your seat."

"Excuse me, I've tried to find out, but I still haven't gotten an answer. Is it normal for the airport to be so deserted? It seems like I'm the only passenger in the whole terminal." I can read the I.D. card pinned over her left breast, inscribed with the name, Ms. Cunningham. However, like everything else that's happened since the first moment I arrived, all I received by way of reply was a half-hearted smile, accompanied by a nod.

It's all been very strange. No passengers. No passersby in the terminal. No companion to share my adventures in the Norwegian winter with or to chat with about the latest news.

I suppose it embarrasses the employees that an international airport should have no traffic. Maybe that's why they don't talk about it.

I feel as if I'm in some artificial theater in Pyongyang where they're required to make you believe everything you see.

I decide not to worry about it anymore and board the plane. The beautiful flight attendant welcomes me, and from the door of the A321 Airbus, leads me to seat 17B.

"But…am I the only passenger?" I ask the attendant, trying to get a response from anyone at all. "Apparently, I've rented a whole plane all to myself! Real adventure travel! My friends at the Polo Club aren't going to believe this," I proclaim loudly.

"You may move up to First Class if you like, Mr. Larsson," the flight attendant says.

By the studied politeness and tone of her reply, I understand that they're uncomfortable with their financial losses or with the general lack of interest in visiting Norway. I'll stop insisting. It's not my problem, but why didn't they cancel the flight?

I'll move up to First Class and put the seat all the way back. I'll order drinks and give them something to do.

I sit down. I sigh. I look at the seat next to me again. This isn't happening…is it? I watch the sad spectacle through the window. The airport workers drive a single luggage cart toward the plane. I can't shake off my astonishment and pick up my phone to capture this absurd moment. Just as I'd planned, I call the flight attendant, ask for a Scotch on the rocks and a blanket. I'm gonna fly like a celebrity!

The captain introduces himself over the P.A. system, "We'll be flying eastward at an altitude of about ten thousand meters. It's ten degrees Celsius in Oslo; no turbulence expected."

Yes, I know, I know. I'll listen to the sexy flight attendant's security instructions.

"The plane has four exit doors. Under your seat, you'll find…"

And so, I get lost in daydreaming about this absurd moment it's been my fortune to experience. Two, three, four…seven Johnny Walkers on the rocks. I rise from the seat and comically begin dancing Swan Lake across the wide aisle of the plane. The blanket serves as my scarf. The flight attendant invites me to sit down and keep my seatbelt fastened.

"Why, Miss? Would it bother the other passengers?" I laugh mercilessly. "Please, could you bring me another little glass of my friend, *the walker?*"

"Sir, please, take your seat while I get your beverage."

"If I take off my shirt, would it be considered inappropriate conduct during the flight?"

"If you don't sit down, that would already be inappropriate conduct, Sir. Don't make me reconsider the convenience or inconvenience of your next drink."

"How about a little kiss?"

"Sit down, please!"

I decide to compose myself and have a seat. Because if I don't, it'll be the only thing I'm having. I take the blanket and cover my torso, closing my eyes. I feel a wave of warmth; there's something burning my back. I wake up on the shore of a lonely beach.

Beside me, the fur coat, a spilled glass of Scotch, and a blue blanket with the embroidered logo of Bloowish Airlines.

Crow 22

Aleja Ventura

The rumbling of the train and the horns honking insanely echoed as he waited his turn before the temperamental traffic lights on the avenue. He'd had enough of all that.

Of the dogs barking at the storm.

Of the kids crying because their bottles were late.

Of the delivery boy who walks down the hallways without stopping to dig in the containers of unfulfilled hopes.

Ten hours of constantly searching throughout Aleja Ventura's world. Wrinkled hands that shorten the distances between what she feels and what she thinks. Deep inside her, those spaces have turned into an outpouring of nostalgia, difficult to sustain. Resistant to everyone's attempted compliments on her lucidity to raise her spirits on those Miami afternoons of casual encounters and floral shirts. It's not easy to collect wise solitude once it has determined to filter silently through the room. An unexpected expert who makes her presence known without paying attention to the passage of the years. Endless, empty, deep on this early morning, surrounded by the coasts of Florida in April 2015.

The ten longest hours of her entire life. How to explain the accordion of madness that hides within time? Too violent to recall that yesterday was many years ago. Too late to acknowledge José Julián's phone call, informing her that he has arrived at the airport. Whimsical curls of contradiction that don't quite manage to divert her glance from the pendulum of the oak clock on the wall, oscillating of its own accord above the decades of patience and menthol left in her mouth. That's how such things work.

Gray hair doesn't grow more valuable over time, though to take pleasure in oneself is an art that few achieve in their youth. It's not in vain that bold denials fill her days with guilt, bathing them in regret, filtering timid cascades of white thread that invade her face, despite her efforts. Only twenty-four square meters of courtroom separate her from this platinum-covered loneliness, a space covered by a tapestry of ancient designs, a worn-out leather ottoman for a bench, and an iron mirror playing the role of gavel.

That ancient anguish, redolent of damp wood, which insists on bringing up raw memories through flashes of what she yearns to remember but cannot. And again, the image of that London clock, inherited by her grandmother when she didn't even have anywhere to live. That clock, eager to mark perpetual conditions of slavery, standing next to the closet wall. The rhythmic swinging of the pendulum doesn't do much to correct the tuneless melodies of anguish above her head. And also, above a pair of sparkling lamps that decide to accuse it, as if searching for answers that will appear only in the cadenced beating of her heart, just behind the elaborate Virgin of Mercy that her husband gave her after their honeymoon in Barbados.

So many leaps, from anguish to galloping expectation, cannot prevent her from noticing the sun's slow farewell through the only window that separates her from a world so different from the one she dreamed about in the Venturas' vestibule, when the donkeys nudged the carts down the streets of Quisqueya, indifferent to the weary animals' cries. Neither will the endless anguish keep her painful joints from disappearing in clouds of ointments and some improvised rags. Sticky blobs of hope that don't accomplish a thing, but at the same time, accomplish everything.

Dresser drawers that smell like burned incense take turns opening and closing, unaware that whatever is in there won't change its essential banality, useless to many, sometimes refreshing for the aching hands of the one who keeps them in the vain hope of clinging to her life in other places, though with the same dreams. Aleja alternates opening them, even though she knows she won't find anything different inside. Maybe the same thing happened years ago, somewhere between Miami and Quisqueya. Who knows if something she's never seen before will now distract her into surrendering helplessly to the edges of the enormous mahogany bed, to the middle of a room that displays it like its most unexpected trophy.

"The upper drawer needs to be closed before the lower one, because then, they look like little sandwiches," she says to herself.

The answers she's looking for aren't there, either. She still doesn't see anything behind the Virgin of Mercy. Because really… Pastor Leonel's rosary, boxes of medicines she no longer takes because it's impossible to check their expiration dates, photos of the old church of San Andrés when she was twenty-two or twenty-three, or twenty—she doesn't know anymore. The fact is, in those days, her knees didn't hurt so much. Nevertheless, hidden toward the back of the rickety drawer, right beside all her souvenirs, is a little red box sealed with sticky tape to keep the highly stimulating, feral concoction from spilling out, a mixture whose purpose she can hardly recall.

And why did they prescribe this for me? she thinks. *José Julián must know. After all, he knows everything.*

Aleja rides to the rhythm of days of long bathrobes and a short memory. A memory that's not as selective as she'd like. Or something like what happened a couple of years ago, when she pretended not to remember anything so as not to have to give explanations. Anyway, the advantages of old age can be selected for one's own convenience, because no one is going to remind her to her face of how many years she's lived, which, for anyone who doesn't know, are almost as many as she devoted to loving Albertino.

For a woman who was so attractive in her day, love affairs can never be forgotten. Long ago, she'd stored all those amours along with her least comfortable outfits. That one, wrapped in a plastic supermarket bag to protect it from dust, stands out from a bureau repaired with carpenter's staples and badly splashed-on white glue. Sequins, lace, and bright colors, which, at the time, lent them special elegance. Today, the plastic that covers it is cloudy from being stared at so often. Today, she's not sure if all those memories are exact, though deep down, in the place where her stubbornness dwells, her dignity in protecting herself from time causes her to suffer mood swings several times a day, obliging her to go along with whatever choices her memory makes.

No one feels sadder than when they always smile. On the other hand, at this age, certainties are treacherous and make her fight with herself. Which is why, without trying too hard to conceal her feelings (because the mirror doesn't worry her), she can leap from irony to common sense, from tears to furrowed brow, from raucous laughter to reality, in just a few seconds. Eighty-six years of inexhaustible experiences don't go by in vain—experiences that remind her that some of her deepest thoughts move more quickly than her legs. Her reflection in the TV screen reassures her of this as it glows from the back of the room, exiling half of the mirror and reducing her to the only resource she has for talking about loneliness and pills. Meanwhile, the delivery boy never stops by to say hello, and the telephone doesn't ring to announce José Julián's arrival to confirm her suspicions.

A forty-five-inch Samsung TV with a smaller rear end than her own was the Mother's Day gift that her only son gave her and later installed, leaving it set on the craft channel.

"These newfangled things are very complicated. They make them with no rear end and complicate them with all those buttons," she says quietly.

But if there's anything Aleja knows how to do very well, it's how to get along with her circumstances, even if she has to spend the day opening and closing drawers. Though, in a strange way, today, her attempts at cultivating a good mood have remained insistently inside the small studio apartment to get through the days bathed in fantasies of everything that today smells of sepia. With walls that balance against the vulnerability of her slow gait. Today, she won't attempt to run away from mischief's temptation, because she really does enjoy frolicking in that delicious taste of pleasant memories.

A painting of the Last Supper hangs above the headrest of the bed, standing out among the old furniture she was given in Santo Domingo after her marriage to the father designated for her son. A good man, that Spaniard. She doesn't regret having spent her years with him. His departure was a little painful. Today, with fewer doubts than yesterday, she recognizes that it was the best life she could have given José Julián. Yes, she lets loose a burst of shameless laughter. The two bags beneath her eyes, laden with years, aren't made for crying jags.

"Aleja Ventura, do you take José Albertino Rosario for your lawfully wedded husband, to care for him and love him, in sickness and in health, until death do you part?"

"Yes, Albertino, I do."

"José Albertino Rosario, do you swear to take Aleja Ventura for your lawfully wedded wife, to care for her and love her, in sickness and in health, until death do you part?"

"Giovanna? What are you doing here?" replies the surprised groom, raising both hands above his head.

And that was as far as the ceremony went. And Aleja's illusions. And the priest's cassock. Because on the other side of the altar, there appeared a blonde with enviable curves and a long mane of curls, who got a rise out of everyone wearing pants in that church, including the priest. A long, yellow gown, swaying to the beat of a stunning figure, whose delicate, bare-arms stood out like the branches of an araguaney tree, showering Albertino with photos, some of them torn, attesting to a secret relationship between her and the groom. Inside the church, all was a chaos of uncontrolled shouting and confusion. Disbelief, coupled with harsh looks on one side and the other. The Venturas were the first to take action, yanking Bibles from the prie-dieux to hurl against the Rosarios. The mother, Petra Rosario, a dark-skinned woman of stylish appearance, but coarse manners, waved her fan because she needed air and because she needed to hide the shame that overcame her.

Grandmother Adelita Rosario, incapable of hearing the arrival of a thousand-elephant stampede behind her without the greatest of efforts, discovered what had happened when Santiaguito shouted into her ear that Alberto had another girlfriend. Only then did she begin to cross herself endlessly, staring up at the chapel ceiling, in prayers that trembled with notoriety, as she loudly begged for someone to push her wheelchair out of the cathedral without her being seen. Meanwhile, Albertino inched his way backward, pleading for forgiveness and seeking shelter behind Father Urquiola, who also backed out of the cathedral toward the cross, astonished by such an assortment of outrageous acts in a single place. And the choir boy! That mischievous little boy who managed only to laugh himself silly, with no attempt to hide his amusement.

Blows, expletives, and expressions of astonishment flooded San Andrés Cathedral. Paquita Rosario, Albertino's sister, watched as her Pekingese got loose and bit Father Urquiola, while the choir boy, before the suffering priest's threatening glare, stifled his laughter by biting his cheeks, just to get the dog off the priest's back.

"Someone get this beast off me! It's possessed by the devil!" Father Urquiola shouted, trying to extricate his cassock from the out-of-control dog's teeth. "You people have come to bring misfortune upon God's house!"

The atrium broke off from the rest of the church thanks to the weight of Albertino, launched there by Aleja's well-delivered right hook, to the astonishment of those few who stayed behind to witness the debacle.

Rosario against Ventura, grandmother against wheelchair, Priest against Pekingese, choir boy against laughter, and Aleja against her urge to hang Albertino by the neck. In the heat of the confusion, though not uttering a word, Aleja never took her eyes off her unfaithful groom or the fluffy-haired, big-breasted blonde.

Now, those days are nothing more than memories. I'd never met anyone named Giovanna in Albertino's life. It might have been any one of the vixens from the stables where Albertino worked, or maybe some random money-grubber he picked up in the bars of Santo Domingo. The fact is, at that moment, Aleja Josefina Ventura could have succumbed to tears and the ruination of her life forever because of Albertino's shameless infidelity. And yet, she didn't do that, because there was Julián Martínez del Rivio, a young descendant of one of the richest landowners of all Quisqueya.

Her childhood sweetheart. He, of the sweaty hands. Julián, that frustrated, confused friend, whose greatest pleasure had been receiving a kiss on the cheek for helping her up from the floor when she fell on her derrière in the old flea market. That awkward nobody, attentive to Aleja's every glance and every reproach, only days before had begged her to cancel her wedding.

"Aleja, don't marry Albertino. I promise to make you the happiest woman in the world."

"Forgive me, Juliancito. You know that I love you, but just as a friend."

Aleja was bewitched by that good-for-nothing, Albertino. A native of San Pedro de Macorís, José Albertino Rosario was like a little chicken with brown eyes, but with a slick tongue when it came to sweet-talking the ladies. A veterinarian by profession, though a con man through and through, Rosario the Hawk, as he was known, had demonstrated, many times, that he wasn't the man for her. But the butterflies in her stomach didn't understand logic. Aleja dreamed of traveling around the world with her brown-eyed, human keyring clinging to her waist.

Because Aleja was huge. A nearly six-foot-tall building that made men swoon by just walking by. Not now, of course, since time has bent her spine, eroded her cheekbones, and knotted her hands with an arthritis that only a glass of rum and ginger, San Onofre, can soothe.

Yes, it was all coming back to her now! When she was twenty-three, the young men of the neighborhood took turns knocking at the Venturas' door and visiting the house on any pretext. Alejandro Ventura, Aleja's father, had a Remington 1100 shotgun that rested on the wall at the back of the vestibule, like a warning to new visitors who might have wanted to take advantage of the Mulatta. Only Juliancito was welcome in that house, or possibly, someone else who had more ready cash than he did. Nevertheless, there weren't many suitors who could satisfy that rapacious family's outsize appetites.

171

"That's what it was like in those days," thinks Aleja with a fistful of photographs in her hands. The families wanted to set their hopes on the best they had. And, for the Venturas, Aleja was the jewel in the crown. Because Jazmín, her younger sister, hadn't turned out to be so charming. Rather, she was more destined to the role of the sister, who stays at home with her parents, taking over the daily routine of a family with limited possibilities. As a result, for Aleja's parents, "the Spaniard" was the ideal man "to better the bloodline." He always wore impeccable white shirts, starched by the Martínez del Rivio's maids. That skinny Spaniard "had what it took," and the Venturas wanted to be a part of it. In fact, the whole family (except Aleja) had made plans to move to "La Martinera," the largest hacienda in the region.

On Sunday mornings, amid family breakfasts and to Aleja's displeasure, table talk revolved around each family member's plans as soon as they had moved to the Martínez's home. They longed to stroll through the thirty acres of fertile land, with stables everywhere, and lots of cash to fund a wedding in the Mediterranean or in Venice, with Greek delicacies, caviar from southern Norway, waiters clothed in haute-couture uniforms, famous guests, and a flutter of high society types whose status had nothing to do with them, so that surely they would have to play the fools to conceal their marginality while enjoying the best view in all of Santorini.

But no. Aleja's heart had settled on a *tinglado de tambora*, a great feast with drummers and other musicians, at the Rosarios' household. With puréed plantains and onions, beneath a heap of mamón, and beer for the guys. That was why, when Aleja accepted Albertino's proposal, her family threw her out of the house. It was pretty hard for the Venturas to understand that the "high society" party was not going to happen. Later on, old Alejandro accepted the deal—fuming and swearing, but he accepted it, nonetheless.

Throughout all of this, Don Julián Martínez wasn't really comfortable with his son's taste. As far as the wealthy cattleman was concerned, his firstborn could have aimed much higher. Who did that nobody think she was, rejecting his son so many times?

Old Alejandro Ventura had tried to ingratiate himself with "the doc" on many occasions, but more than once, they had left him at the door of "La Martinera" with the bottle of rum and the fine Havana cigars that he bought with a whole month's salary. More than a gift—it seemed like an offering to his much-revered in-law.

"What a mess with Doc Martínez. He must be very busy. Tell him I'll come tomorrow." And off he would go, his cowardly face downcast and his serenade postponed for another occasion.

For that reason, on his wedding day, young Julián thought his world was ending, because he didn't even want to dress appropriately for the occasion. Sitting in the last row of the church and reeking of cheap rum that quarreled with his social status, he tried to hide his joy at the commotion that the appearance of the so-called Giovanna had created. After all, he had offered Aleja everything, from thoroughbred horses to very expensive jewels and perfumes that smelled like refined people and that could be found only in the best fragrance boutiques of Paris. But she was dazzled only by the smell of Albertino's cheap patchouli whenever he showed up drunk in the wee hours to regale her with serenades and other idiocies typical of the Hawk.

"I'm pregnant by Julián!" Aleja shouted, laughing ironically in Albertino's flushed face. "Is that what you wanted?"

"But Aleja, my love, you know that all this is a misunderstanding. You know…"

"Father Urquiola, I'm going to marry Julián. Today, I'll give him the wedding night that this unfaithful sinner doesn't deserve," she said, picking up the train of her wedding gown.

"And you," pointing to Albertino. "Go away, and let that slut drag you off to hell, but Aleja Ventura will be married today, and it won't be to you!"

"By the holy power of Christ's blood! What are you trying to do, girl? Marriage is a very serious thing," added Father Urquiola, horrified.

But what does it matter to change things around on a whim? Money had always been the prime mover for the Martínez del Rivio family, and of course, Father Urquiola wasn't about to be the exception that afternoon at the church.

"Is it true what that girl is saying, my son?" Don Julián Martínez asked his son, trembling but undaunted.

"I'm afraid so, Father."

After a deep sigh by the wealthy farmer and a couple of glances exchanged with Doña Carolina del Rivio, his wife, he proclaimed, "Well, then, there's nothing more to say here. A Martínez del Rivio must always fulfill his responsibilities, no matter what the cost."

After a long talk with Father Urquiola, while the choir boy cleaned the incipient wounds on his left leg with methylene, the cleric agreed to officiate at the wedding.

How much did Old Man Julián pay? No one ever found out.

That hat-sporting Spaniard was one of the main contributors to any cause championed in Santo Domingo. Which meant that he could buy anything, up to and including the church, if he so desired. As a result, it wasn't long before the Rosarios were kicked out of the cathedral, soiling themselves with fear, taking the dog, the wheelchair, and the blonde with them.

The frightened Venturas didn't know whether to celebrate the Rosarios' expulsion or flee the church through the back door so that no one would see them, thanks to the scene Aleja had made and also because, even though she would marry "the Spaniard," Old Man Julián had made it very clear that all the business about the wedding was merely a matter of obligation and to honor his family name. There would definitely be no shrine to haute couture in Santorini, nor any flamboyant feasts. Besides, the Venturas wouldn't be welcomed in "La Martinera." Old Man Alejandro was even more disappointed when he learned that his plans to become the big boss of the countless stables had all gone to hell. Because Don Julián was a man of his word, but he was no fool. And even less was he the type with enough humility to mix with the Venturas. That was one thing he understood very clearly. In fact, he was giving up a lot to save his son from the immorality of the woman who was about to take his name, though let's not fool ourselves, he also broke down when he saw his son dragged into church by a woman. Juliancito had always had everything. That woman might be just another toy for him, though later on—to everyone's surprise—Julián would turn out to be a good father to JJ.

Nevertheless, tragedy decreed that the makeshift love affair would not endure. Julián had an accident in a riding contest in Miami and died when his mare, Bailarina, crushed her rear hooves into the back of his head like a bag of popcorn. By that time, Aleja had become a very cold, distant woman, the kind who count their steps so that no one will know they've arrived at a given place, which was why she made all the arrangements for a tacky, ostentatious, and unforgettable funeral. She was very interested in letting everyone—especially Old Man Julián— know how important that man had been to her. Over time, she had learned to love Julián, though not to such an extent as to clutch the urn and ask to be buried with him, especially since she was quite aware of all the properties and goods that would pass into her hands after that gold-plated urn was sealed.

The brilliant glow of the coffin loudly demanded the attention of all those attending the wake. The more eyes there were on the luxurious event, the fewer would focus on Aleja and her discomfort at not being the conventional widow, the kind everyone hopes to see rending her garments and drying her tears at the foot of the open casket.

During those ten hours of waiting and remembrance, during which she was able to recall moments of nostalgia while sitting on the edge of the ottoman, Aleja understood that her son was in the proper hands, which led him to become the best civil attorney in all of Florida.

A graduate of Yale Law School, José Julián Martínez was born in the United States, where he grew up wrapped in luxury that he otherwise might never have enjoyed. Now, Aleja had been widowed, inheriting a large cement business and other properties that, as one might expect, she would be unable to run correctly. José Julián had been at the head of those businesses, which didn't necessarily mean that they would be better run.

An inveterate gambler, the Martínez heir, had bankrupted the cement plant in the casinos of Las Vegas, Monte Carlo, and New York. Married to Alice Gibson, a nurse from California, who went with him everywhere (on both business and pleasure trips), attorney Martínez del Rivio, as he insisted on being called, ended up becoming a TV personality. In his expensive TV ads, he invited viewers to call him if they wanted to make a pile of money in all kinds of civil suits, which, of course, ultimately fattened up no bank accounts except his own, thanks to negotiations that he customarily carried out behind his clients' backs. Afterwards, those clients had to pay him 40 percent of what rightfully belonged to them. Lawyer stuff.

On the other hand, Aleja paid for the Venturas' vacation trips, Caribbean cruises, and other whims in Santo Domingo, where they eventually moved to a very comfortable mansion on the outskirts of the city. Their squandering was of epic proportions. They spent so much that soon, the widow was begging Old Man Julián for a loan to salvage the cement plant.

"You can count on the fact that my nephew will never lack for anything, but as far as you professional spongers are concerned, you won't touch one more peso of my fortune."

Aleja had always thought she had Don Julián by the balls, because the Spaniard adored that ne'er-do-well grandson of his, even more than his own fortune. However, after that harsh conversation, she realized it wouldn't be so easy to manipulate the father-in-law, and so, her next move was to sell the cement plant and invest the little they had left in a small restaurant in northwest Miami.

It was never the same again. Of course, that is, assuming they wanted to live the same life as before.

Today, these things are only memories. And Aleja, tired of waiting, had no qualms about telling all of it to the TV set, as if it could reply. "You can't touch that machine too much because the channel changes and José forgot to set the remote control," she said aloud, with her phone in her hand.

Her phone, of course. Another device she always picks up with her hands, cracked by the impudence of a time she hadn't noticed passing by. It could have been turned off. Or maybe it was damaged, because José Julián said he would phone her as soon as he arrived at the airport. As coincidences have been a constant in Aleja's life, they've shown up again today to make the phone ring insistently, perhaps at the most inopportune time to take a call. Her blood pressure pills, even when cut in half, are still too big for her to swallow with a single sip; therefore, she tries to put them back into her pillbox.

At dusk on an afternoon filled with budding joy, her movements are nervous and rushed by the desire to receive the phone call.

The pill and the phone at the same time. Her mind can still respond, but her hands cannot. Gone are the days when she could do two or more things at once. The pills have fallen to the floor of the small apartment, and she won't be able to find them until JJ comes, because her knees don't bend as well as they used to. The ringing of her phone also stops, not allowing her time to answer the call. Now, sitting in her torn leather chair, cracked by the threads of fire filtering through the window, she tries to pick up her tortoise-shell-framed bifocals resting on the nightstand by her right hand. Her movement is faulty, and so, she tries to get up from the chair, urging her knees on again, straightening her hips and knocking over the Virgin beside her date book and dozens of instructions to remember.

But her bifocals aren't there, nor are they on top of the refrigerator, nor behind the toilet seat cover. They simply aren't there. And now, she needs to find out where she left them, but first, she realizes that she's wearing them.

"And I thought I had lost them... This mind of mine..." says Aleja out loud, stifling her laughter to keep her dental implant from falling out. Her mischievous joking is interrupted by a new ringing of the phone.

"Hello, José?"

"Hi, Mom. He arrived, and we're on our way to the apartment."

"That's great, Son; is everything all right?"

"Yes, Mom, everything's fine. We had a few mishaps that slowed everything down, but at least we're about to arrive."

"How wonderful, Son. Well, here I am, waiting for you. Now, I have to look for my blood pressure pill that fell on the floor and I can't see it. And it seems like that TV set has changed channels all by itself. I don't know. You know I don't understand much about these things, but I can't look at my craft channel. I also have a broken little box of pills in the drawer, but I don't remember what they were prescribed for. Do you know what they're for? Because if you don't, I'll throw them away. Heaven help me if I get them mixed up one of these days."

"Yes, Mom, don't worry. When I get there, I'll organize everything that needs to be done. A red box, you say?"

"Yes, Son. It's at the back of the drawer, covered with some papers that look like airplane tickets. I don't know because I don't see well. These glasses are kind of loose. But I'm worried because I don't remember if it's a medicine I need or not. Imagine, so many times I've opened that drawer, but I've never seen that box before."

"Don't touch that box, Mom. We'll take care of it when we get there. And another thing…don't mention this to anybody else."

Aleja always listens to what José Julián tells her. If that box mustn't be touched, well, there must be a good reason. Although she finds it strange, because she has absolute control over what goes into and comes out of that drawer. It doesn't matter. The boy will soon come to resolve all pending matters.

And since ten hours are often insufficient to wait for answers from life, the knocking on the apartment door rang out very loudly to announce someone's arrival. Maybe the pharmacy delivery man.

"Miami Police! Open the door!"

Aleja had never imagined that her world could change so much after those knocks at the door, because the police entered the apartment with an arrest warrant that would end up capturing her days of nostalgia. It was to be expected that old Don Julián, in addition to knowing how to pay off Father Urquiola, would also know how to pay the best private investigators to look into the vile murder of his only son. A macabre plan that all of them were involved in, Aleja Josefina Ventura Torres, who wanted to get rid of Julián forever, as well as José Julián Martínez Ventura, the famous attorney-cum-gambler who wanted to get his hands on the inheritance as soon as possible and who, besides, had never intended to visit his mother on that afternoon of fruitless waiting; and Señor José Albertino Rosario Mireles. Yes, that predatory veterinarian who had secretly administered a strong dose of stimulant to the mare, her nervous system quite affected, which had thrown Julián to the ground, only to discharge all her weight upon his skull.

Nevertheless, and most important for Albertino, he had wreaked his vengeance against Old Don Julián Martínez de Rivio, the powerful ranch owner, who had paid a shapely whore named Giovanna to tempt him in a casual, but premeditated way, and thus, take the photos that would put an end to Albertino's happiness on that afternoon in the Church of San Andrés.

Crow 23

Ludovico

I hear a shot fired in the room.

I strike the chair with both hands and get up, frightened.

It's been a long wait. Ludovico has avoided me ever since I returned to save him. And now this? Up to what point can a son be independent without his father feeling guilty?

"I killed her and closed the door," said Ludovico, half out of his mind, after tossing the anguish-stained murder weapon onto the carpet. "I see that you haven't gone yet, even though you left me all alone."

"And why should I have gone? You broke the eyeglasses when you decided to take that woman's life!" I shout, overwrought and trying to calm down. I consider that it might be better to lower my voice and take control of the situation.

"If I were you, I wouldn't have done it that way, but I understand that the passage of time and my absence have taught you to make your own mistakes."

"Where is it written that I should pay attention to you now? You show up whenever you want. Of course, you abandoned me minutes after I was born—me, the product of your rape of that lying bitch. Or have you forgotten that?"

"Ludovico, don't insult your mother like that! What do you know about death when you've barely been born? Baby face! You've struggled with your own ego ever since you experienced the horrors of a necessary desertion. You never had the right to keep me at your side. I couldn't stay there, and you know it. You entered this house to kill Grace, the woman

181

who fed you when your steps were still wobbly. What kind of piece of shit does that?"

"You think about it. What kind of piece of shit did you turn me into?"

"I tried to avoid it, and that's why I'm still here, asking you and asking myself: Where did I fail? The body is lying over there. And what do I do with that now?"

"It shouldn't worry you. You left her before you left me. You could have abandoned her again and let life take its own course. I'll keep doing my part, while you hide like the coward you are. Behind your protection is my desire to put an end to this story. Kill me if you have the guts."

In the face of that challenge, I throw up my hands. In a way, Ludovico is right, though I'll never accept it. In the aftermath of his baseless trial is my desire to say, "The hell with everything," including him. I will never forgive what he did with Grace. For God's sake, she was his mother! It's true that I never loved her, but it wasn't rape. It was just passionate sex in which a "no" turns into a "yes." It's just that the "yes" wasn't so explicit.

Afterward, I used her to flee the scene, but it was for other reasons that don't concern that useless fool. I know what you're thinking. I, too, am a piece of shit. But I'm a different kind of piece of shit. I didn't kill her. Or did I?

"Ludovico, I'll make you a deal. I'll let you escape as you please. Live the life you want to live and stop being a psychopath tormented by the abuse of your childhood. I'm offering you a second chance."

"A second chance What do you want from me? Do you want me to kill you, too?"

"No, Ludovico. I deserve it, and I get that loud and clear. But someday, you'll understand that resurrecting your mother is the most convenient thing for both of us. I have the power to do it. That way, you'll be able to go on without guilt over the cruel murder, and I'll free myself from the guilt of being the Johnny-come-lately father of a beast who should have never been born."

"So, will you give me the chance to kill her again?"

"Boy, you are a real bastard. But at least you're an interesting bastard. Your coldness forces me to tell the story of an infinite hatred and to demonstrate my despair as a grieving father."

After this conversation, I return to the armchair from which I shouldn't have arisen.

Ludovico Alcántara, the main character of my novel, will now be able to strengthen his perversion in the madness of a drama overflowing with the craving for revenge.

Crow 24

The Phantom's Revenge

Hello. My name is Lux, and I'm invisible. I discovered this when I was sixteen.

I may have been standing next to you at the supermarket or while you were taking a shower. I have to accept it…I like being close to you. That's why I've chosen to call myself The Phantom. Although I'm not the typical ghost who's died and whose soul wanders around the darkest corners of reality. No, that's not me. I've seen quite a few of those, and if I were you, I wouldn't worry about them so much. Those jerks don't even know where they are. I, on the other hand…You probably don't want to know, but I'll tell you anyway.

I know the secret you want to find out, whose it is, and—yes, I admit it, I've also been to the Beyond. I've crossed the portal of what is morally correct for those who are visible because there are no rules in my world. I've always been the same, a marginalized being who has built his own reality for the eyes of those who have driven me away. Isn't that the history of Messianism? I've accepted it.

Without further ado, let's begin with the only thing that matters, for the one who writes this message to you is the owner of the world.

From the time I was a child, people were constantly connecting me to strange head wires, subjecting me to all sorts of tests, and gnawing my mother's health insurance to the bone, even to the extent of losing her job to provide me with care for a special condition invented by society to justify my presence in it. Later on, she could no longer keep paying the insurance premium. The doctors never came to a conclusion that would satisfy their long-winded scientific speculations, and then, they started over again. Hospitals, the press, insurance companies, psychiatrists, lawyers, pharmacies, laboratories, and even the school turned us into a festival of humiliations that designed the reality they so richly deserve today.

My mother died three years ago of a tumor that couldn't be treated properly because she dedicated time to me and to not exhausting her insurance. The scavenger birds at Saint Pliny Hospital, instead of accepting the fact that I was developing an invincible power, made me spend my childhood taking large doses of antihistamines and other stuff like that.

My hygiene was very poor. At school, I was called "Deodorant Lux" and, of course, I was excluded from everything that required other people to come near me of their own volition.

"Children, quiet please. We're going to assign partners for the science project this week," said Ms. Marta, our teacher.

And after calling roll and pairing off almost all the students, the teacher said: "And you, Carlitos, will work with Lux this week."

"Miss, why does it always have to be me?"

"Carlitos, we've discussed this before. Lux is a classmate like anyone else, and Karina did it last week."

And that's how she integrated me socially. That's what it was like with everything. I remember that for the end-of-the-year dance, I had to pretend I had an injured leg to keep my mother from suffering when she saw that none of the girls wanted to be with me. As a result, my first kiss happened at the same time I lost my virginity. Not everyone can say that, and for me, it was a big deal. I was seventeen, when I could already be invisible enough to do whatever I wanted—in this case, to drug a famous Hollywood actress in a suite at the Hotel Ritz and possess her until I was exhausted.

In fact, I'll also make a confession. Many times, when someone doesn't remember what they did the night before, I was there beside them, having some fun and doing what I know how to do best: remain in the shadow of my miserable loneliness.

Aquagenic urticaria was the doctors' pronouncement.

As they couldn't find any explanation, they went for the easiest possibility. Doctor Fabricio Orzuela, a stubborn, bald, and solitary old man, reached this diagnosis since my skin couldn't tolerate contact with water. Only twenty assholes in the entire world have been born with this strange allergy, and that idiot thought I was one of them. I really think the guy was one of those who goes to brothels to find a wife. The idiot lived at 30 Lunas Artes Street, and he drank a lot. I grew tired of peeing in his whiskey, as he was the one who raised the flag of that aquagenic shit. He participated in TV interviews, medical forums; he sold books and even wrote an article for Scientisse magazine, in which he was described as the self-sacrificing doctor who headed the medical team treating my condition. According to him, my life was improved thanks to his brilliant intervention. Journalists congregated in my house to get a scoop. It was so ridiculous that I ended up making a TV commercial for a famous brand of mineral water. "El Paraíso mineral water. Even I like to drink it." The commercial ended with Dr. Fabrizio's advice and his famous statement, "I recommend it, too."

Poor fool. I was your king, your Messiah!

As the years slipped by, water only functioned as a catalyst to speed up the process of cellular mutation that would guarantee my absolute transparency, for which I needed only to take a shower in order to emerge from the bath like an invisible Adonis that touches everything, sees everything, hears everything, and therefore, controls everything.

I discovered that the recurring nightmares, like the incessant muscle pain I suffered, had a purpose in my life: to be the Chosen One. I'm the one who only needs to achieve omnipresence to reach the highest rung of celestial consciousness.

It's hard to hear this, but life is full of things you don't want to hear; even so, you keep going. Now, I've begun my work on earth: to rid it of all the rats that cause our fellow beings' suffering. For the time being, I've achieved the death—under "strange circumstances"—of all those who have made my life impossible. We'll see who's next.

My life is dedicated to the spiritual mission with which I was charged. The realization of my legacy must be known not only by you, but by everyone who breathes around you. As one might have expected, the writer of this book didn't notice my presence, nor will he ever notice it. He'll keep thinking that the typing noise he hears while he sleeps is the product of a deep, healing dream, which surely will give him some idea to write about the following day.

Another fool.

During the day, I construct my stories, and at night, I go to the writer's house to empty out the dreams. Through his book, I will tell you of my deeds, and of course, of the end of each of my hangmen.

Do you want to know what I did with each of them?

DR. FABRIZIO ORZUELA, NEUROSURGEON

Well, I didn't really screw this one. To tell the honest truth, it was the Mafia that fucked him over.

I discovered that he provided prescriptions for Gino Spinatto, the famous drug dealer. The owner of half the town and even of the underwear Fabrizio wore. In fact, that creative baldy was the doctor of the entire Spinatto family. So, it was that I later understood many things.

How can a local doctor enjoy the luxury of driving a Bentley Continental GT?

At a simple office visit for a common cold, Dr. Fabrizio "made a mistake" and prescribed a prostate-specific antigen for Il Capo.

And to control a Mafioso's sneezing? Well, the good doctor "had the idea" of removing Mrs. Spinatto's red lingerie from her bathrobe pocket and offering it as a handkerchief to the disgruntled killer. Poor Fabrizio Orzuela. Professional idiot. Deep down, he was the one Spinatto liked best because of the candies he kept in his office. That was why, before the Mafia submerged him in a container of acid, I made him donate all his ill-gained possessions, including the beautiful red Bentley, to the man who had divorced his daughter three years earlier. Life doesn't get more splendid than that.

Now, shall I tell you about the psychiatrist?

No, better not. Let's leave the sex addict for last and that way, we'll add a little order to this story. Meanwhile, give me a minute, because the lovely redhead in high heels has stopped right in front of me. Ooh, how nice she smells! The breeze blows her skirt up. She smells heavenly. She's texting a man, telling him to get ready for tonight because she's shaved. Liar! For sure she's about to run home to do it right now.

Did you know that redheads aren't red down there?

I'll pay her a visit later. The reason for the visit? I'll explain it to you later. Now that I'm thinking about it, I'd better follow her, because I need to slip into her house with her. Let's return to those judged by the Phantom in a little while. Okay?

JAIME COLÓN, PARISH PRIEST OF THE ALCORTA JUÁREZ CHURCH

Here comes the father. The old guy seems like a good person, though I caught him in a few iffy dealings. Besides, he thought my "evil possession" could be cured by bathing in holy water while praying sixteen *Our Fathers* and fifteen *Hail Mary's*. The screams I uttered during the ritual could be heard for five blocks around. He lived in the church at the corner of 33rd Street and Alcorta Juárez Avenue, and he told my mother that he was the right person to carry out the exorcism.

You have no idea how I laughed by making the cross fly from his room like a balloon and walking his cassock around the room even though the door was closed with lock and key. I also wrote him a message on the mirror that said, "Praying won't help you." Before his heart attack, the priest climbed into bed and started spitting out prayers, along with his dental plate. After he died, I dressed him in women's clothes, and that was how the altar boy found him, with glitter on his ass and a five-speed sex toy leaping all over his bed.

189

May his remains rest in peace, and may God receive him into his bosom.

Vicente Lutero, village healer

The one who read cards and tobacco. The one who launched snails. The one who made your partner return to you in three days and three nights. The one who talked with the spirits.

He made my mother prepare a mixture containing a cat's tail, parrot shit, and the seeds of a rare tree that could only be gathered on a mountain, which could be reached after a five-hour walk. I had to drink that stuff before beginning the ritual.

Makalakakum ayé… lomimama arekum malakuna.

May all the spirits of the Beyond hear me and make the Evil One leave Lux's body!

The diarrhea was relentless.

I told my mother that this was the unmistakable sign that the forces of evil were leaving my body and that they would do it little by little, in about ten sessions that cost two hundred dollars apiece and with a bottle of Indian jujube rum as an offering to the spirits.

I must confess that I did think about it a little. It couldn't have been from a fright because I was going around drunk, and in such cases, revenge loses its flavor. A bullet to the forehead would have been too quick. And so, I had the idea of adulterating his drinks with small doses of an undetectable laxative. And that included the water he drank to rehydrate after each bowel movement. Before he died, he received a note that read: "The Evil One had trouble coming out this time, didn't he?"

Carlos C. Carrizales, my former stepfather

He made my mother's life impossible. Let's not waste too much time on him, since he committed suicide. I wasn't able to find out the cause of his unforeseen sexual impotence. He also wasn't too thrilled to discover the reason for his inexplicable hemorrhoid problem. The toothpaste wasn't going to help him with that, right?

The doctors thought he was gay, but they didn't want to mention it at his appointments. I think he decided to hang himself when he received some photos of himself asleep without underwear.

GINA PULITSOVA, CLINICAL PSYCHIATRIST.

At last, we arrive at the top of the list of wretches, who have been sentenced by the merciless Phantom. I need to end with this confession because the redhead in heels is just about to arrive home.

Gina, Gina…

Trying to manipulate a young boy into accepting a condition he doesn't have was abuse, at the very least. Confrontational therapies to make me overcome my fear of water were not, similarly, events to be appreciated. However, I fell in love with you, and that's why I follow you now. I've always followed you. That beautiful red hair has never left me in peace.

"What do you want to do today?" Gina asks me.

"I don't know. My invisibility today has been boring."

"Let's go visit a friend. It'll be something special for you."

"The man you were writing to before?"

Gina laughs. "That's part of the surprise."

"You know I've never liked threesomes."

"It won't be anything like that."

I never expected it. Gina has brought me to the house of the writer, who has now decided to publish my story.

Crow 25

Pocaterra

I joined the caravan, not suspecting that on that March afternoon in 1918, I would finish the story of all my returns. In my tight, black gabardine suit and top hat, its brim raised toward the peak of my authority, I advanced with the haughtiness of one who parts multitudes as he walks along. Because, when all is said and done, I am the owner of Pocaterra. Commander in Chief. General. Lord of lords. El patron, as they'd say in Casa Cristal, the government seat of a town that still lacks stories to tell about Don Ayala.

What if everyone loves me?

I'm not so sure about that, but they'll soon learn to. Hunger is a good teacher, and time will bend the knees of some of the troublemakers. Today, I've departed again, but this story is different. Health is a serious business, and the people need their leader to be in perfect shape, with the unbreakable voice of authority and a firm pulse for spreading it throughout these lands.

"Julita, you know what you have to do, because if we neglect to do it, Pancho will beat my butt!" I said to the woman who was always at my side.

With her head down and her hopes squelched, Julita nodded half-heartedly.

"The whores are getting to me," I grumbled, as I felt what was left of my virility start to burn. Dr. Pérez-Mitre has warned me about it, but I wasn't going to let myself be dragged around by some bar girl from the Pocaterra pool hall.

"Celestino, c'mere, Son!"

"Yes, my General," replied the presidential guard.

"Get the boys ready and tell them to fuck up Acosta for me if he keeps acting like a fool."

"Everyone around here does whatever I want! There are lots of clear-eyed folks who think that Don Ayala won't come back to these parts," I said, glaring at Pancho Gomera.

It was just a moment before I heard the required outcry of the masses, and with a clenched fist and my glove on high, I bade farewell to what—until today—had fit neatly into one hand.

"You never know, Celestino. Pass me the rum bottle so I can take a shot!"

"But my General, remember that Dr. Pérez-Mitre—"

"Pass me the bottle, goddammit! Can't you see I've got the gringos breathing down my neck and half the town whispering? I need clarity so I can think! Or do you want to stay in Pocaterra, milking the cows?" I yelled at Celestino, joining the astonished Julita.

"At your orders, my General!"

Seventeen days had passed since I'd had to name the lawyer, Pancho Gomera, as second in command, and I didn't feel at all confident about abandoning the chair. I haven't told you this, of course, but the chair is what people fight for most of all around these parts. Everybody wants it, and Pancho, as some Christians from Casa Cristal call him, is one of those who would kill to sit his butt down on it. However, the thing some folks call "political diplomacy" led me to seat him nice and close to me, in an effort to get the gringos to see the thing with different eyes. After all, I would be moving the strings every time I breathed, and the liberal conspiracy had been dismantled at gunpoint by the presidential guard, combined with rum and cash. In Chirimoya, they're conspiring with the gringos, and even though they pretend not to notice, I know that too many cooks spoil the broth.

Distaste aside, the trench coat grew tighter as the car rocked back and forth, just as my conversations with Julita had been growing stronger over the past three days. My dazzling companion, in her elegant white dress, still tried to reject me with her gaze, by tipping her hat to one side, and inserting her filigree fan between us with feigned contempt. Stopping the car with each brush of our hands. Pretending to be on the right shore.

What a piece of work that Julita is! I thought, in the blink of an eye…

I didn't want to believe the stupid gossip buzzing around Casa Cristal, but Celestino knows that if Julita and Acosta were meeting with Pancho Gomera's ballbreakers, all of Pocaterra would find out, as clear as glass, that you can't fool Don Ayala that easily. For the time being, my trip led me into the hands of Dr. Pérez-Mitre, who tried to risk his life in an operating room in Paris. Because I'll never die, especially not when someone grabs me by the balls. And yet, after the lights in the operating room were turned off, I wanted you to know who Lucio Martín Ayala really was. The warlord who took up arms in the town of Pocaterra and who now, with the advantage of being anywhere and nowhere at the same time, is going to take off his top hat and go searching for the bastard who sold him into Pancho Gomera's greedy hands.

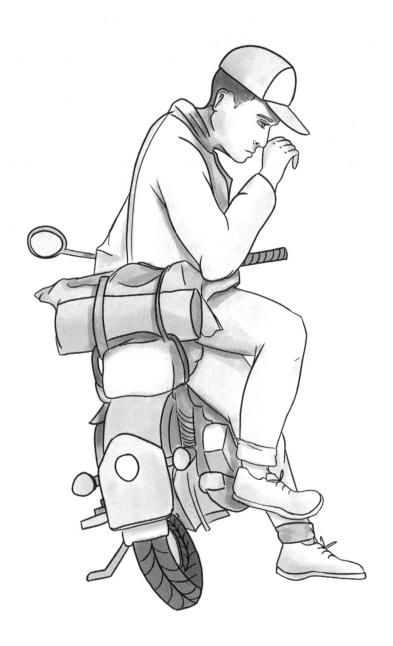

Crow 26

Lanky's Helmet

I fell, dejected, at his feet.

Minutes earlier, my legs, refusing to take responsibility, had pretended not to recognize the road that lay before them. I needed to keep going, and so I did. I didn't count my steps, nor did I multiply them. The stress of the day weighed upon my back, my eyelids, and my desire to do anything. I had awakened at 3:00 AM to get to my math class at 7:00. An hour to get ready and eat a few crackers. An hour to reach the terminal at Maracay. An hour standing in line to board the bus. An hour's walk to campus.

An hour-long battle, drawn in shreds and pieces, awaits me.

I've put on the wrong socks! Should I sit in the back row of every classroom? I wouldn't want anybody to suspect that I have no other socks. The fact is, I can't tell colors apart at this hour of the morning, partly because of the lack of light, partly because I'm asleep, and partly because I don't have enough socks.

I'm on my way back now, though somewhat held up by traffic on the Downtown Regional Highway. A fatal accident near the Cabrera Tunnel allowed me an extra hour of sleep, which I try to complete in my bed before starting out on my next excursion. My last transportation today— or at least, so I think—has left me a few blocks from my house. I start walking the rest of the way.

"Wuzzup, Juancho?" I ask the scruffy gangsta.

"Hey, buddy, still eating books?"

"That's right."

"This skinny dude works his ass off, not like you, a bum who spends all day with a joint hanging outta his mouth, and a lowlife. Take it over there, Lanky, we wouldn't want the guys in Block One to get it wrong," Juancho says to his squatting sidekick.

I check my watch. It's 11:10 PM, half an hour later than usual. My makeshift bodyguard stubs out his cigarette and revs the engine of the little motorcycle, which now has become my last ride of the day. I hop on because I know it's my only option. I don't want to be unfriendly to a group of gangsters, nor do I want to lose my calculator to a vagabond pothead. You can't help thinking about it, but on these roads, being the friend of a bunch of delinquents isn't a choice. It'll never be my choice, anyway, and besides, I'm already sitting on the motorcycle.

I adjust my fear and my backpack. I take Lanky's helmet.

"Put on the helmet, bud. If I get fucked up, it doesn't matter. It'll be one less burden, but a future engineer of the Republic? No, Sir. Like I told you, if you don't finish your degree, don't show up at home anymore. The old lady deserves at least one useful kid. Meanwhile, I'll go buy the medicine," says the foul-smelling criminal, extending his arm behind him as a sign that I should hand him something.

"What about you? Have you ever thought about getting your life together?"

"Nah, bud, books ain't my thing. My college is life. For example, what college teaches you that the piece of shit dressed in blue flannel who's crossing at the corner is involved in some kind of con? So, hold on, bud, because that guy is a member of the Block One gang and we've got a couple of scores to settle with him." Lanky hits the gas pedal on his beat-up Suzuki 125 as if it were a high cc cycle racing against a fearless type who points to him, makes the sign of the cross, and quietly condemns you with lips pressed together and brow knitted from the adrenaline rush. Regardless, Lanky insists on keeping his hand extended backwards and directing a few words to me.

I get the message. Now my hands—and my life—start to shake. My breathing speeds up to previously unknown rhythms. The desire to cling to Lanky was the same one that screamed at me to get the hell off that motorcycle. Without asking for it, I find myself in the midst of a war between killers, when the only thing I've managed to steal were a few kisses. The man in the blue flannel stops around twenty meters in front of the motorcycle and sheds his undershirt like someone preparing to face off with the devil.

Lanky skids the motorcycle with an ability that only inhabits those touched by evil, and he unsheathes a nine-millimeter chrome *Beretta* that I didn't even see emerge. Now, I'm face to face with the man from Block One who, unfortunately for me, manages to fire first.

The bullet pierces the helmet.

The bullet also pierces time.

It seems my son hasn't arrived. Early in the morning, I hear the brass door shut, and from that moment on, my thousand daily prayers begin. Yesterday, I saw him arrive later, and all I hope for today is the possibility he'll come home earlier, for his peace of mind and my own. I never thought a father would want his son to quit school, but desperation has never been a friend of common sense. Anxiety has given me strange dreams these days, and yesterday, I woke up with a start because I saw him in the middle of a shootout, a kind of anguish I don't wish on anybody.

These have been very rough times along the back roads. The gangs have declared war for control of the zone. I'm going to wait for him on the avenue.

It takes fifty seconds to get from the front door of the house to the point where it intersects with the public byway. A half-smoked cigarette is the only thing that goes with me. I'm barefoot. His lateness is very strange. Right now, what worries me most is a bare-chested man, standing with a piece of blue flannel in one hand and a weapon in the other. The insolent shot forces me to let go of my worn-out traveling companion. The cigarette hits the ground at the same time as the head of that boy in the black helmet. One man lies wounded on the sidewalk at the feet of the first, and my son's backpack is visible on top of the spinning wheel of a motorcycle I don't recognize, and which splits my life into a thousand pieces, absorbed by the bullets of desperation. The man from Block One runs toward the cycle like a bird of prey whose turn has come and fires the weapon three more times at the poor wretch in the black helmet.

I fell, dejected, at his feet.

Minutes earlier, my legs, refusing to take responsibility, had pretended not to recognize the road that lay before them. I needed to keep going, and so I did. I didn't count my steps, nor did I multiply them. The stress of the day weighed upon my back, my eyelids, and my desire to do anything. I had awakened at 3:00 AM to get to my math class at 7:00. An hour to get ready and eat a few crackers. An hour to reach the terminal at Maracay. An hour standing in line to board the bus. An hour's walk to campus.

I fell, defeated, at the feet of Lanky, who just a moment earlier, had stretched out his hand to ask me to give him back his black helmet, the one that brought him miserable anonymity.

"Buddy, give me the helmet! When a thug goes to war, he doesn't show his face, and if that punk is looking for trouble, it's gonna be me, not you. Hold on tight. This ain't no math problem!"

Lanky is dead. His old lady's medicines and my old man's despair have disappeared along with him.

Crow 27

Letters in the Darkness

Time of death: 7:36 PM.

You might think that everything that's tossed from a sixteenth-story window is destined to be thrown out. Maybe she was the one who ruled out the majestic balcony of the Le Séjour Hotel, ending up hanged beneath the fine artistic touches of a Monet. Five stars that will become four as soon as the cover pages reveal the photo of the impressive penthouse, cordoned off as a result of the scandal.

A fine English silver tray with still-warm leftover food beneath her dangling feet. A half-consumed glass of Dom Pérignon, with lipstick stains on its rim. The detective's suspicions suggest that she couldn't have done it herself, and the security cameras record only one person's access to the room: Janeth, the unluckiest Algerian chambermaid in all of Paris. Nevertheless, during a three-minute lapse, those same cameras were deactivated. That troubles the police, but not Detective Duboix, the first to arrive at the Dantesque scene.

He walks through the room and strips her naked in search of answers. He seems contorted.

An appointment book emerges from among the fine silk Eiderdown, suggesting a meeting related to the French Ministry of Health. There isn't much to look at, nor does he want to do it.

He's concentrating on the correspondence received by the guest on that warm July afternoon. Meanwhile, Janeth, her hands covering her face, only remembers that at the time of the grim discovery, she was handing the mail to Dr. Luisa Harden, who is now a possible murder victim.

Eight black envelopes, still sealed, are sent to forensics until they can be opened by judicial order. Traces of saliva as well as some bite marks on Harden's breasts add to the confusion. At the hotel, the employees are shaken by the news, and the guests try to abbreviate their stay. The noise of doorknobs turning blends with that of luggage being dragged along the corridors, while the visitors scatter in all directions, vying to get to the packed elevators first.

Whispers. Confusion. Everything is in chaos in the gigantic lobby, now that the police have forbidden anyone from entering or leaving the hotel.

"You can't do this to me. Don't you people know who I am?"

"Terribly sorry, Monsieur Phillips, but these are police orders," the receptionist explains.

"How can a thing like this happen at a hotel of this caliber? What sort of people are you letting in?" replies the famous Irish sculptor, banging on the reception counter with both hands.

Additionally, the police have ordered a check of every room. Now, the luxurious privacy has been invaded by agents who stop to interrogate possible witnesses and try to untangle some clue that might lead them to a clarification of the facts.

"I was sitting on the sofa in the lobby when I saw some very strange gentlemen walk up to the entrance of the hotel," declares Madame Colbert very nervously, covering part of her mouth with a white silk handkerchief.

In the hush of the dark ambience, all the guests have received eight black envelopes, identical to those that were found in Dr. Harden's penthouse, and those who have already opened them agree that in all of them, there appears the name of Frederick Duboix.

"Detective Duboix?"

"Yes, that's me."

"I'm officer Juliet Durant of the United Federal Antiterrorist Unit of the National Police. We need to ask you some questions about the Luisa Harden case," the official explains, flashing her I.D. with her left hand.

"Imagine, the feds have arrived! Don't you think that suspecting a terrorist attack is the same as falling into the game of a sick murderer?"

"There's no murder yet, Detective, unless you know something we don't. All we have is a body hanging from the ceiling. And we also have two hundred eighty-eight identical envelopes with your name written inside. I don't know if you're aware of that. Every message contains a letter that, in itself, doesn't seem to mean anything, but which, combined with the letters of the other messages, in a terrifying phrase, might be directed at the occupants of the hotel: 'YOU'RE NEXT.' Do you have anything to tell us about that?"

"Juliet, what I have to tell you is that right now, we could have a murderer in this hotel, trying to rack up another victim while you and I keep playing Sherlock," Duboix counters in a hurried attempt to end the conversation.

"And that murderer could be anyone, including you."

"Dammit! Are you accusing me, Juliet?"

"No, Detective. But you'll have to provide an explanation for this video that shows you entering the hotel twenty minutes before the time of death. Do they teach some kind of ESP in the Homicide Division?" Juliet argues as she shows the screen of her smartphone to Duboix. "Did you know the victim?"

"I don't know what you're talking about. I arrived at the scene first, after the phone call from headquarters since my unit was closest to the hotel. They could have tampered with the videos, or maybe with something in the square heads of the antiterrorist unit. Isn't that a possibility?"

"Yes. In fact, everything seems to indicate that the videos have been tampered with. And with regard to that, one female witness attests to seeing you enter the camera room of the hotel at 7:15 PM. What were you doing there, Duboix?"

"Who is that witness?"

"So, now, we have to reveal a witness' identity to a suspect? Tell me about the black backpack you held in your hand. What's in that back-pack?" Durant insists. "Also, tell me about that photo where you're seen at a restaurant with Doctor Harden two nights prior. Detective, I'll repeat the question. Did you know the victim?"

"This is pure nonsense!"

"I don't think the situation lends itself to your refusing to answer, unless you'd rather talk at headquarters."

"First, accusations, and now, threats. I hope you know what you're doing."

"Detective Duboix, you'll understand that we must relieve you from this investigation and take you into protective custody. Come with us, please."

To protect his privacy, Duboix is led through the back door of the restaurant to a special cell at General Police Headquarters, some ten long blocks from the hotel. At that moment, it starts to rain, and Juliet isn't at all comfortable with the detective's arrest. There are good, solid reasons to avoid handing a suspect over to those in charge of the investigation of a possible terrorist threat. You can assume any content for the backpack, including the mysterious envelopes, with the aggravating circumstance that he deliberately lied about his relationship with the victim.

Frederick Duboix, long-time expert in explosives from the Sûreté Nationale, was being investigated by internal affairs regarding suspicions of cooperation with Algerian terrorist groups during the attacks on the Champs-Elysées in 2017. Juliet was trying to find a connection between Duboix, Dr. Harden, and these terrorist groups, and up until now, hadn't been able to do so. Not much is known about Harden, only that she held a doctorate in biochemistry from the University of Johannesburg and was in Paris to deliver a lecture about bioterrorism, invited by the Ministry of Health.

Two-and-a-half hours have passed since the chambermaid found Dr. Harden's body.

Now, Juliet has been summoned to the hotel lobby.

The anti-explosives unit had found the black backpack on the ceiling of one of the elevators, and therefore, the building needed to be immediately evacuated. It's true that, during the evacuation, the murderer could have escaped—camouflaged—among the crowd. Regardless, the lives of hundreds of people had to be safeguarded.

Evacuation protocol is carried out to the complete satisfaction of the guests, along with the establishment of a three-block safety perimeter around the hotel. At the same time, anti-bomb equipment is approaching its objective. The elevator is deactivated, and the specialist from the Special Actions Force very cautiously begins his descent on the elevator pulleys. The lights twinkle inside the cavity, limiting vision.

The humidity is overwhelming, while outside the security perimeters, a handful of reporters, passersby, and rubberneckers await a sign that might unravel the spectacular news.

The specialist has reached the backpack.

His tense, sweaty, gloved hands move hesitantly before making the decision to approach the shiny zipper, not without first hiding himself behind the tested security harness.

Duboix finds himself isolated. Desperately, he cries out, asking them to let him out, but his pleas will not be heard until he clears up his connection with the facts. Despite it all, he pounds the bars, declaring himself innocent and shouting that there's an error which he cannot explain right now. The press speaks of a murder and of a possible explosive device in the hotel, for which the French government has initiated diplomatic dialogue with its Algerian counterpart. Terrorist cells had been detected in France since 2005, and presumably, some security organizations are infiltrated.

Meanwhile, at the hotel, the backpack is opened, and the unexpected occurs.

A million euros in cash is transferred by the police to the forensics lab. Juliet asks to interrogate Duboix immediately. Why did he enter the hotel with such a large amount of money? It's very late.

Duboix is discovered hanging in his cell. At his feet lie eight black envelopes, similar to that mysterious mail at the hotel, though this time, the name mentioned in the letters is that of Didier Harden, the one-year-old son not recognized by the hapless detective.

After a few days, Duboix's phone was examined by the police. The calls made by the detective revealed his five-year romantic relationship with Dr. Harden.

In addition, a public communication from the terrorist group, Algerian Immortality, took credit for the murders for refusing to collaborate in the development of a biochemical agent for the terrorist cause, which is why Duboix and Harden's child had been kidnapped.

Duboix was to pay a million euros to a contact known as Janeth.

A lethal and very contagious virus has been transmitted via the two hundred eighty-eight mysterious envelopes.

Crow 28

Two Rocking Chairs

When you plant something, it's not just a seed that's germinated. A hope also grows. That's what my Abuelo says when I visit him at the farm on Sunday afternoons. The handmade sign that hangs above the corroded red pipes on the front door warns visitors that they cannot enter without an invitation: "I'm only interested in my dog's teeth, not what he rips with them." No one gets close.

Very few people have seen the dog. However, it's not hard to imagine Tweety's merciless face. A purple pitbull, weighing around seventy kilos, and with two flamethrowers beneath his mutilated ears. He has scars on his face and also on much of his body, as a result of intense battles with ocelots and other predators that try to steal Abuelo's chickens.

When we arrive, and even though Tweety knows us, we prefer to wait for Abuelo to tie him up so we can come in. Then, my dad and my uncle get out of the car so that together—each one at one end—they can open the front gate. During the rainy season, they have to pull it from underneath to unlock the pins from the puddle. They do it by themselves because Abuelo doesn't come out to welcome visitors. Never.

Sitting about twenty meters from the entrance to the farm, he makes a sign with his thumb to let us know that Tweety is tied up. In fact, that gesture means several things at once. On the one hand, it shows that Abuelo okays the visit. On the other hand—and the sign that everyone understands first—it shows that the damn dog is under control. But also, it's a clear indication that visitors should deal with the gate by themselves, because Abuelo doesn't budge from the rocking chair to greet guests. If anyone wants to come to the farm, it's their own decision. In this part of Puerto Santo, people really appreciate spare communication and the solitude of the countryside.

With me, Abuelo talks a little more. I'd say he practically turns into a poet because he says I'm the family's hope; that is, he thinks I should be the one to take over the farm when he's not around anymore. This is no minor matter, either. It's like the line of succession, as close as can be to an inheritance to the farm's crown. My Abuelo feels like part of the farm's royalty, and this property is a great palace covered with mangos and pumpkins. The real problem is that my dad, just like my uncle and aunt, Alberto and Sonia—the youngest—left home before they were eighteen. They ran away, I mean. With little bags in their hands, they caught the only bus that would take them away from the town, old Farias's "El Chicharrón," a Ford 750 with a converted platform, but not comfortable enough to avoid swallowing a mouthful of dust. Everyone who wants to get out of Puerto Santo and go to the capital has to make use of "El Chicharrón," unless you're a member of the Rodríguez family, because those guys have their own trucks. In other words, mere mortals. "El Chicharrón" leaves the market in town every day at 7:00 AM, when the morning is nice and cool. But getting off "El Chicharrón" isn't the end of the line. After several transfers, overnights along the route, casual pick-ups, or long walks, you finally reach the capital. And that's what my grandpa's children did—in other words, my dad, my aunt, and my uncle. I think there wouldn't have been so many problems if they had gone somewhere else. Cienpinta or La Ensenada, maybe. But Abuelo hates the capital as much as he hates visitors. At age seventy-something, he may have stepped foot there three times, according to what he himself says.

"If I go to that place, it's just to renew the papers for the farm."

And why doesn't he like the capital? It's a mystery. Old man stuff. Some memory that affected him when he was young. I don't know. The fact is that he hates it so much that he checks the daily papers to allow himself to trash talk everything that goes on there. If what's going on happens to be good, he says that the capital has the same things as towns like Puerto Santo. And if it's bad news, then he claims that that's the reason he won't go there and fill himself with misery, because the misery of the capital sticks to you. He can spend the whole day sitting in the wicker rocking chair, ranting about something he read and watching anybody who passes by the front gate. It's obvious he doesn't like visitors.

I remember how one time, a guy who sold pots and pans tried to convince him to come over to the gate. Abuelo just made that sign, but a negative one, with his index finger.

I imagine that doing his sales training, the poor guy was told never to accept "no" for an answer. He opted to insist, but he was mistaken. *If Mohammed doesn't go to the mountain*, the unfortunate wretch must have thought.

The outcome? A prosthesis for the place his right leg once occupied.

"If the man doesn't know how to read and doesn't understand words..." my grandpa said.

And imagine: They came after him with lawyers, letters from the capital, and he even got a note from the prefect of police, but Celso Molina is a very shrewd old guy, clever in responding. No taller than five-foot-two, his skin tanned from planting so many seasons of crops, and strong as an oak. Anyone could be fooled. Although the old guy was a refined type, there's no way to change his nature. Reflective, a man of very few words, and a lover of his shrubs and his dog. Say anything to him. Insult him if you like. But don't step on the grass or throw a stone at Tweety. Don't think folks around here haven't tried. Behind that rocking chair with a few loose cords and his peaceful, countrified appearance, there's a rifle and a great determination to use it. That's why Abuelo has no friends.

"Goddammit, Celso, your beast fucked up my monkey!"

"Look here, Pancho, it's best if you round up your animals and don't let them come here and fuck up my property. My dog doesn't leave the farm, so if your monkey shows up in pieces, it's because he tried to pick my oranges."

"Okay, Celso. We're not gonna see eye to eye on this. Let's just leave it at that, in the interest of peace. But take care of that tyrannosaurus of yours, because if I find him in the wrong place, I'll blow him to bits."

That day, Pancho Rodríguez ran like never before along the tractor path. Abuelo followed him with clean shotgun blasts because nobody threatens Celso Molina's Tweety.

"Dad, you've got to keep that temper of yours under control. No one will come and help you when some shit happens here. How could you think of firing at Pancho?" asks my Uncle Alberto, emerging from the bathroom.

"Let that idiot run. Besides, I wasn't trying to kill him, just shake him up a little."

"And what if he has a heart attack? Are you going to bear the weight of that death on your conscience? Or do you think it's easy for a guy that age to run from a shotgun?"

"The monkey messed up my oranges. He destroyed the whole tree! But that's enough about that. From the gate over there to where we are, the law is on my side."

Two branches and three oranges. That was what was missing from the plant. But both Abuelo and Tweety watch over the farm as if it were a nation at war. In fact, the red gate is like the customs office standing before hostile enemy land.

Sometimes, I think my dad, my aunt, and my uncle go to the farm on Sundays to make sure the old man hasn't gotten involved in some craziness. Because he likes women, too, and he doesn't hold back, even if it's someone else's woman. If she stops in front of the gate, is wearing a skirt and has pretty legs, from his rocking chair, he'll offer her oranges, tomatoes, and even flowers from the patio. It's not the first time Abuelo has gotten into it with Pancho, because in addition to fighting over the dog and the mangos that fall onto one side or the other, they've also done it over women.

"Look, Celso, what about those tomatoes you gave Yesenia this morning? You're very chatty with my wife," Pancho shouted from the gate.

"Did I stop at your gate to give away tomatoes?" Abuelo asks, looking up his daily newspaper. "If you don't want me to chat with her, you talk to her. It seems like your wife needs to talk with a man."

And again, the fight resumes. Those two never get tired of arguing. Though Grandpa doesn't win them all. Because Pancho Cortés has money and a bigger farm. At some point, Pancho won a dispute against Abuelo over two fighting cocks. On another occasion, he got involved as a food provider to some small markets in Cienpinta, for which Abuelo had been a distributor for several years. As Pancho's production expanded, he lowered the price of pumpkins by half, and Abuelo's harvest rotted. He did it to wear out the old man's patience, because Pancho doesn't deal with small retail businesses. The Rodríguez family and their patriarch are the great distributors in the capital.

And just when bags of fertilizer, animal feed, and pesticides from the capital began to grow scarce, Pancho brought to his farm truckload after truckload of products that he had obtained on the black market, while Abuelo got by as best he could. There was some kind of war, or I don't know what; the products began to disappear, and without products, it's impossible to maintain a farm. Those were very difficult days.

Abuelo suffered a deep depression that made him hide from the rocking chair. He was about to lose his crops, and besides, some animals began to pay the price for his lack of attention. My father, my aunt, and my uncle did the impossible to find feed for the chickens, along with pesticide to prevent the plague from burning away the sowing. But their isolated attempts only served to calm the situation for a couple of days or even a week, perhaps. Everything turned into small cycles during which Abuelo was overcome by sadness. Days of happiness when Tweety, the goats, and the chickens ate. Darkness when the bags disappeared from the barn.

Abuelo managed to sell a classic car that he had left in the shop for repairs to two mechanics from the capital who had been trying to persuade him for a while, at half the price they had initially offered, because, well, that's the misery that goes along with everything that comes from the capital. Just the same, he had to sell it to pay off the costs of the black market. Despite the timeliness of this solution, it lasted only three months, and the business of the war threatened to last a long time before they would be able to detect some distant bright spots on the horizon. We all thought that Abuelo was drying up along with the farm. Things grew tense, because my Uncle Alberto, in a desperate attempt, tried to convince him to sell the land to Pancho and come live with him in the capital, but Abuelo only threw him out of the house and didn't let him back in again. They fired very hurtful remarks at one another, and Abuelo even grabbed the shotgun. Uncle Alberto couldn't believe what he was seeing; so, he left the house swearing he'd never look after Abuelo again—a typical example of the cure being worse than the illness.

Then, Abuelo began to drink heavily. Tequila by the bottle. When he was sufficiently wasted, he would ask someone to kill him and bury him on the ranch, like fertilizer. My father and my Aunt Sonia, very frightened, decide to move to the farm. For a while, they took turns living there, while Tweety spent his days tied up, eating the bones of the dying chickens. Poor Tweety…he no longer barked. He had lost the grandeur of earlier times. The debacle advanced very swiftly, and after a few days, Abuelo no longer wanted to get out of bed.

It fell to me to remain at his side, telling him stories of beautiful farms and endless pastures where he rode on horseback like a majestic foreman, admirably prosperous. Abuelo laughed. The joy of the open range twinkled in his eyes. I couldn't see him like that anymore. I felt like I was dying with him.

Something had to happen. The unexpected had to happen. And on purpose or not, it happened.

Three truckloads of product arrived at the gate of Abuelo's farm, with Pancho Rodríguez at the head of it and thirty-some farmworkers. We didn't want to tell him. But Pancho demanded to see him as a condition of the deal.

"Dad, we want to tell you something," says my Aunt Sonia, who, as the spoiled child, was the one chosen to try to convince him.

"Yeah. I heard all the noise. Who's out there?"

"Who do you think, Abuelo?" I interrupted, taking his pale hands, bruised from so much work and so many years.

"What do you think I should do?" he asked me, as we all stood there in shock, nearly speechless.

"You should leave, shake that man's hand, and accept a loan. Seal the deal with the word of Celso Molina," I said with all the conviction I could muster. "When you plant something, it's not just a seed that's germinated. A hope also grows. You taught me that. Now, go out there like the brave grandfather you are and sow reconciliation so that true friendship can grow."

Abuelo looked at everyone in the room and tried to pop up from the bed, like a spring.

My aunt and my dad tried to grab him. Abuelo stopped them in their tracks and ordered them not to try to help him get up. He would attend to this business by himself. Stumbling and dragging his feet, he left the room and headed for the front door of the house. He peeked outside, and we followed him. We stopped in the middle of the living room. I stood in front of my dad and my aunt. The old man, illuminated by the sun, placed his left hand like a visor, while the right leg kept him upright against the wooden door frame.

Pancho and my Uncle Alberto were outside, on the other side of the gate. Abuelo turned his head and looked at me. He looked at me like never before, directly into my eyes. I couldn't return his gaze for a long time.

"What about Tweety?" he asked me, his voice broken.

"He's tied up," I replied.

Abuelo lifted his thumb in a sign of approval.

Pancho smiled. Everyone did the same. From that moment on, we always had two rocking chairs at the entrance to the farm. One for my Abuelo and one for Pancho Rodríguez.

ANDREA G. LABINGER (translator) has published numerous translations of Latin American fiction. She has been a finalist three times in the PEN USA competition. Her translation of Liliana Heker's *The End of the Story* (Biblioasis, 2012) was included in World Literature Today's list of the "75 Notable Translations of the Year." Gesell Dome, Labinger's translation of Guillermo Saccomanno's *Cámara Gesell* (Open Letter Books, 2016), won a PEN/Heim Translation Award. Her translation of Patricia Ratto's *Proceed with Caution: Stories and a Novella* (Schaffner Press, 2021) was featured in The New York Times's "Globetrotting" section of notable works in translation for 2021.

WILL CANDURI was born in Caracas, Venezuela and immigrated to Michigan, USA, where he currently resides. He earned an undergraduate degree in Industrial Engineering from the Universidad de Carabobo (Venezuela) and a master's degree in Administration and Leadership from Central Michigan University. In 2021 he published his first book, the best-seller *Ensalada de Cuervos* (Crow Salad). He is also the author of other successful titles, including *Siempre Joven* (Forever Young), *El Misterio de la Garra del Oso* (The Mystery of the Bear's Claw) and *Adiós, Oviedo* (Farewell, Oviedo).

His versatility in writing creatively in many genres, a deft command of scenarios, the solidity of his characters, and his unmistakable, unique narrative tone, are hallmarks of his work.